PUDDLES IN THE LANE

PUDDLES IN THE LANE

Alan Parker

STAR

A STAR BOOK
published by
the Paperback Division of
W. H. ALLEN & Co. Ltd

A Star Book
Published in 1979
by the Paperback Division of W. H. Allen & Co. Ltd
A Howard & Wyndham Company
44 Hill Street, London W1X 8LB

First published in Great Britain by
G. Whizzard Publications Ltd, in association
with André Deutsch Ltd, 1977

Printed in Great Britain by
Hazell Watson & Viney Ltd, Aylesbury, Bucks

ISBN 0 352 30327 1

For Annie, who hates war stories but likes children.
Well, except other people's.

CHAPTER 1
FANCY MAN

If you looked down Paxton Street in September of 1940, apart from the odd pile of sandbags and brown sticky tape on the windows, you would never know there was a war on.

The sunlight cut through the misty autumn air and shimmered in the shallow puddles that had formed, over night, in the worn-down dips of the Victorian pavement.

Curiously, whoever invented pavements could never have known that they were also inventing Hop-Scotch. In Paxton Street, next to Tin-Can-Tommy, it was the favourite game. The chalked-out squares followed the jagged jig-saw cracks of the grey pavement stones that lined each side of the cobbled street. A small gang of children huddled around it. In peace-time there would have been many more, the air would be thick with a dozen friendly arguments—and it would take forever to get your turn. But not now. The war had been going for a whole year and most of the children in the street had been evacuated, far away from the bombs, to the safety of the countryside.

Vee Harris, a pretty blond eleven year old was next to go. Her real name was Veronica but when she was born her sister Joyce, older by two years, could never get her baby teeth around the name, so she had called her "Vee". And Vee she had been ever since. She was also called "Ronnie" by her school friends and sometimes, by Wib and Freddy, her young brothers, she was called "nickers". It goes without saying she preferred Vee.

At the side of the hop-scotch, her brother Wib Harris sat comfortably in a wicker armchair he had taken from a nearby bombed-out house. He wasn't too keen on games and always declared himself "umpire" or some such title. Other children sat around on make-shift seats made from sandbags, borrowed from the wall the A.R.P. men had built around the corner shop.

"You're next, Wormy," shouted Sheila Dexter. Her father owned the fish shop, so she always shouted louder than anyone else.

"Wormy!" The other kids joined in.

"I'm coming. Keep your hair on," said a skinny boy, playing five-stones on the kerb. He had a pale, thin face that was topped off with a haircut Mr Willcock, the barber, called his "Threepenny-all-off". Wormy's slate slid into the square. He was called Wormy because he once had "worms". The other kids weren't sure what this meant; it might even have been one of those words grown-ups use when they don't want you to know something. But whatever it was that "worms" meant, it had left him with twisted knees that always seemed to collapse half way up the hop-scotch.

"Trod on the line," shouted Vee and Sheila

Dexter.

"I didn't," Wormy protested.

Wib got up from his umpire's chair and lifted up Wormy's foot. There, sure enough, was the tell-tale chalk mark.

"Sorry, Wormy. Rules is rules."

At the other end of the street Siddy ploughed through the puddles on his battered red tricycle. At five years old he was the youngest of the Harris family. The wet wheels weaved intricate patterns that criss-crossed the pavement cracks, until Siddy got so dizzy he toppled over. He picked himself up and rubbed his eyes. The dizzy spots cleared just in time for him to see Mr Pollock striding towards Paxton Street.

"Copper! Copper! Pollock's coming."

Mr Pollock was the local special constable who looked after Paxton Street, and had taken it upon himself to police the area for any indiscretion that hindered the war-effort; playing around with bits and pieces scavenged from the bombed ruins came into this category.

The news of Pollock's arrival was of special interest to Siddy's brother Freddy, who was at that moment upside down, half-hidden inside the pig-bin.

"Oh, bloody heck," he shouted. Inside the bin his muffled voice sounded like someone talking into a megaphone with a sock in it.

Ten years old, Freddy was the next youngest after Siddy. He was a quiet, sullen boy—he was also Wib's twin brother. Wib was the elder by twenty minutes; a noisy, chatty individual who took it upon himself to be the spokesman for the two brothers. Consequently Freddy rarely spoke unless it was really necessary.

The reason he was upside down in the dustbin was to secure some dinner for Darkie, a shaggy-haired stray dog who had made his home with the Harris family. The contents of the pig-bin however were intended for His Majesty's pigs and not black mongrels with big appetites. The dog licked his lips as Freddy sorted out a nice, juicy tit-bit from amongst the potato peelings and discarded cabbage leaves. Mr Pollock's arrival had brought the prospect of an early dinner to an abrupt end.

The kids by the hop-scotch scattered in all directions. Wib threw his wicker chair into Mrs Ockshaw's garden and in seconds, he, Freddy, Vee and Siddy had disappeared inside No. 8 Paxton Street.

Joyce Harris would always remember the first week in September. For a start it was Vee's birthday on the first, war broke out on the third and their dad walked out on them on the fifth, two days later. That was just over a year ago now. His leaving hadn't been a lot of fuss, no big row or any screaming and shouting. He had simply put his hat and coat on in the hall, popped his head in the front room and said: "Toodle-loo, kids, I'm off."

Vee, Freddy, Wib and Siddy scarcely looked around. They thought he was probably going to the Hare and Hounds. But Joyce was the eldest and knew differently. She was the only one who said goodbye. Weakly she had murmured, "Bye, Dad." She wished she'd got it wrong. She wished she hadn't heard them rowing through the thin walls that divided their bedroom from their parents'. She wished she could have got up and run down Paxton Street and said, "Please don't go, Dad. Come back." But she knew it would just prolong the unhappiness between her mother and father. It certainly would be hard without him, but at least there was a chance her mum might start smiling again; something she hadn't done for ages. The neighbours had assumed he'd joined the army and Mrs Harris never let them know any differently.

The whole family were going to be evacuated at the outbreak of war but Mrs Harris had wanted to stay in London. She was a Londoner after all, and she had a good job at the Co-Op that she wasn't going to give up lightly. As for being parted from her children, it was out of the question. Her husband walking out on her had made her cling to her family all the more. One separation in her life had been enough. But since the heavy bombing started in September, she had begun to have second thoughts.

Violet Harris looked at her lined face in the cracked mirror that hung on the back of the scullery door. There was very little powder left in her compact and she rubbed the last of it into her ageing face. It helped a bit, but not much. Since the abrupt departure of Mr Harris, she had forced herself to go out.

"War or no war," she would say, "Saturday night is Saturday night—and I've still got to enjoy myself. I'm not getting any younger."

Joyce took the fish and chips from her newspaper and divided them up on to four plates, keeping the remainder in the paper for herself. It was nicer out of the newspaper; the vinegar seeped into the newsprint and gave the fish and chips a flavour all of their own.

In the tiny scullery, Vee pulled the chairs up to the table and puffed up the cushion on the seat so that Siddy could reach his tea. Wib opened a Player's Navy Cut tin and took out a bundle of picture cards, which he neatly laid out on the table. Vee bit into the crisp piece of fish.

"This fish is all batter."

"Mine's all right, don't be so fussy," snapped Joyce, as she popped half of a delicious looking onion into her mouth.

"Why have you got an onion and we haven't?"

"'Cause I went down the fish shop and queued up for it, that's why, clever boots."

Vee shrugged and looked over Wib's shoulder at the neat rows of picture cards. Not being able to get the better of Joyce, she had a go at him.

"You've got two the same." She pointed to two cards that Wib had laid down. They were both pictures of footballers. Both players had their arms folded. Both had flat, expressionless faces and greased down hair swept clean off the forehead, with a side parting so straight it could have been cut with a razor. Wib didn't even bother to look up. He took a deep sigh to indicate his sister's ignorance of such matters.

"They're not. To you they look the same but that's because you know nothing about picture cards and nothing about football."

If there was one thing Wib knew about it was cigarette cards. He always kept them in the metal Navy Cut tin with two elastic bands wrapped safely around it. He would religiously read the backs of the cards, with the consequence that he was not only a champion cigarette card flicker, but also a walking encyclopaedia of useless facts like, "Who scored the winning goal in the 1932 Cup Final" and "Who scored the most number of sixes in a Test Match". Vee vainly persisted in trying to outsmart her brother.

"Well, they've even got the same shirts and shorts."

Wib sighed once more. "One's Bolton, one's Fulham."

"They *look* the same."

"The badges are different. To you they look the same 'cause you know nothing about it." Wib's thick Hackney accent spat out the words that spread all over Vee and shut her up.

At the other side of the table Freddy shared his tea with Darkie, who had sat patiently, safe in the knowledge that a nice, greasy chip would eventually come his way. Darkie was Freddy's friend most of all. That's not to say he didn't get on with the rest of the Harris family. But when it came to those freezing winter nights, when the air was so cold it made your breath look like steam from a kettle, Darkie would single out Freddy in the dark bedroom and snuggle up to his warm body beneath the blankets.

"Here, Darkie." Freddy threw a chip up and Darkie snapped it out of the air with the skill of a trained circus performer. Vee had aroused Joyce's interest in Wib's picture cards and she too began to pore over the neat rows. She pointed to a sepia picture that Wib had placed separately from the rest.

"What's that one?"

"That one's special."

"What's so special about it?"

"'Cause it flicks the best."

Joyce gingerly picked up the card, under Wib's suspicious eyes. Certainly it was a little thicker than the other cards, which no doubt accounted for its special flicking qualities. The sepia image had started to fade slightly with age and constant flicking. But there was no mistaking who the lady was.

"It looks like Mrs Johnson from upstairs," said Vee.

"It *is* Mrs Johnson," confirmed Wib. "She gave it to me ages ago."

"That's right," said Joyce, looking up from her fish and chips, "it's when she was a young girl in the music hall. 'On the boards' she calls it. I think she was a dancer or something. Mind you, I don't know how she managed it to look at the size of her. If she danced now she'd probably fall through the stage."

Vee laughed at Joyce's joke. She always did. It was the best way of getting on her good side so she could stay up a little later than the boys.

Mrs Harris came into the kitchen with a cluster of hairpins clenched between her teeth. She tucked her pink blouse into her skirt, licked her finger and stroked her eye-brows. Her make-up was now complete. The powder had covered up the wrinkles a bit and the lipstick that she'd given a shilling for on the black market had turned her pale, thin lips into two passable rosy-red Cupid's bows.

"Right. I'm ready. Is everybody O.K.?"

Wib jumped in quickly. He knew his mother always felt a little guilty leaving them on a Saturday night and with the bombs as bad as they were; it was a chance he couldn't miss.

"I'm still hungry. Is there anything else?"

"Anything else?"

"To eat."

"Like what?"

Normally, he wouldn't have dared to ask. "Like some ice cream?"

The question wasn't as daft as it sounded.

The Paxton Street residents were lucky in that Mr Palermo, who had an ice cream stall in the high street, mixed up a mystery concoction of powdered milk and flour in a lock-up garage right opposite the Harris' house. Everyone had long since forgotten what the real stuff tasted like, and if they pestered him enough they would come away with a free jug-full.

"Joyce, do him some bread and jam," snapped Mrs Harris, ignoring his request for something tastier.

"There ain't no jam," Joyce replied.

"Then do him some dripping. There's some left in a basin at the back of the larder."

"I don't like dripping. It makes me sick unless I have salt on it." Wib knew when he was on to a winner.

Joyce opened the cupboard door and took out the basin of dripping. "I'll put salt on it, don't worry. Just close your eyes and pretend it's jam."

Freddy threw Darkie another chip, which didn't please Mrs Harris at all.

"Don't give your tea away, Freddy. You're skinny enough as it is. Soon, if you turn sideways nobody'll be able to see you."

At that moment little Siddy dozed off and, but for the nice plump cushion Vee had sat him on, he would probably have fallen headlong into his fish and chips.

Mrs Harris tucked her hair behind her ears to show off her gold-coloured ear-rings.

"Right. I'm off. Joyce, you know what to do. You sure you'll be all right?"

"Course we will." Joyce looked up at her mother who fiddled with the buttons on her coat.

"I hate leaving you. But I won't be gone an hour. An hour and a half at the most—and Mrs Johnson will be upstairs if you really need anything. Remember, Joycie, you get them down the shelter as soon as you've finished your tea. And Freddy, I don't want you messing with that dog. Wib! Don't pick your nose, love. How many more times have I got to tell you. Proper turns you off your dinner—and you'll get nostrils like the Blackwall Tunnel, mark my words."

Wib took his hand away. It was a constant disappointment to him to be born with such small nostrils and such exceedingly fat fingers.

"Bye, Mum."

The Harris kids said goodbye in unison. As Mrs Harris turned and walked down the passageway, she looked back briefly at Joyce. It was a tiny look, but Joyce caught it and knew what it meant.

Vi Harris slammed the door closed behind her. No mother should have left her children with the air-raids as bad as they were. Joyce knew it and her mother knew it.

As a rule, Freddy never spoke much, because he didn't need to. Anyway, with Wib around it was impossible to get a word in edgeways. For the moment however Wib was silenced by a large mouthful of bread and dripping, so Freddy took the opportunity to ask a question.

"Why does Mum go out on a Saturday night?"

"To go down the pub."

Unfortunately Vee's answer wasn't good enough.

"But the pub's been closed for months."

Everyone knew that. They'd even closed the Odeon for a while in case a bomb hit it. Vee tried to put their minds at rest. She was older than the boys and kidded herself she knew a little more.

"She goes to see someone."

"Who?"

"It's a secret."

"You mean you don't know," countered Freddy.

"Course I know. She goes to see Uncle Stanley. He lives down the pub and he's Mum's fancy man."

At this Joyce threw her screwed-up fish and chip paper at Vee.

"Watch your lip, Vee. Don't go telling them things they don't know nothing about. 'Cause you're not supposed to know, either. It's a secret. You shouldn't have told them. I won't go telling you no more secrets if you're going to open your trap every five minutes."

But it was too late, because Freddy's interest had been aroused. He had a cheeky, puzzled little smile on his face.

"What's a fancy man?"

Wib, informed as ever, quickly gulped down his bread and dripping to offer an explanation.

"Don't you know? It's a man who . . ."

Joyce felt like stopping him by stuffing his bread and dripping down his throat; but it wasn't necessary because the air-raid warning sirens did the job for her. The chilly wail cut through the night air with an evil familiarity and filled the Harris scullery with fear.

CHAPTER 2
THE RIVER OF ICE CREAM

They all looked up at the ceiling, except for Siddy who had fallen asleep in his plate of chips. Joyce grabbed him in her arms and started shouting instructions.

''Freddy, get your eiderdown. Vee, bring the dominoes and Siddy's woolly. Wib, get the black bag in the sideboard.''

The Harris kids obeyed her every command. In three weeks of bombing they had become very used to it, and for the first time in their lives they did what they were told. Wib ran into the front room and took the black bag from the sideboard. In it were all the Harris' valuables. No jewellery or precious gems, just the ration books, identity cards, Government leaflets, and four neatly-folded pound notes Vi Harris kept for a rainy day.

Out in the back yard Vee helped Freddy pull his bed quilt through the door of the Anderson shelter that had become their second home these last few weeks.

The small corrugated iron shelter was tucked into the corner of the tiny garden, in between the outside lavatory and the adjoining wall they shared with their next door neighbour, Mrs Ockshaw. There was just enough space for the six of them if they snuggled up close, with a bit more elbow room on a Saturday when Mum was out. It had been great fun at first, like a secret hide-away; a game of cowboys and indians and this was their camp, huddling around a single candle that was their log fire. But as the bombs had got closer and louder, their game of make-believe had been spoiled by the hideous sound of ack-ack guns firing blindly into the night sky.

Joyce ducked down to negotiate the tiny shelter door. In her arms Siddy was still fast asleep, despite the bombs.

Freddy and Vee snuggled under the grey blankets.

''Where's Wib?'' Joyce shouted. ''Wib, get in here.''

Wib replied from the scullery.

''I'm getting the gas-masks.''

He appeared with a pile of gas-mask boxes in his arms. As he pulled back the entrance curtain he tripped on Freddy's foot, and the boxes toppled to the floor.

''Pull your feet in, stupid.''

''Sorry, Wib.'' Freddy apologized to his other half.

The corrugated iron roof of the shelter curved over them, making them feel a little easier. Although it didn't soften the sounds of the bombs, it was cosy, and once they'd been under the covers for half an hour or so, it got quite warm.

Vee stacked the gas-mask boxes neatly at the

end of the shelter. They hadn't had to use them so far but they'd been told at school to take them everywhere they went, and it was always a comfort to know they were close at hand.

Wib laid out his picture cards by the light of the flickering candle that Joyce carefully balanced on an old saucer in the middle of the shelter. Freddy snuggled up with Darkie and Vee emptied the box of dominoes on to the blanket. Siddy suddenly stirred in his sleep. For one horrible moment Joyce thought he was going to wake up and get irritable. She breathed a sigh of relief when his restlessness stopped.

The first bombs of the evening seemed to fall a long way away, but the vibrations still rattled the shelter, making them seem very close.

"Mind! You're leaning on my cards." Wib pushed Vee away from him. She ignored his rudeness; he was always like that about his picture cards.

"I wonder where Mum is, Joycie," said Vee. "Do you think she's in a shelter?"

"Bound to be—or a cellar maybe." Joyce reassured her sister and, in a small way, herself.

"Pubs have got big cellars," offered Wib. "That's where they keep the beer. I went down a cellar once when they were delivering at the King's Head. They're fantastic places with hundreds of barrels and crates—and it stinks something rotten."

"That's 'cause it's underground," said

Freddy. "Dampness always smells like that."

"No, it's not. It's the beer. It stinks of beer. 'Orrible it is."

The raid soon passed. It hadn't been a very bad one because Joyce and Vee had got through only three games of dominoes, and both Wib and Freddy had joined Siddy in the land of snooze.

Vee too began to yawn. She pulled the blanket over her shoulders and put her head beside Joyce on the uncovered pillow.

The eerie after-raid silence soon beckoned them both to sleep. In the distance the "all-clear" sounded the official end of the raid, but neither of them heard it.

Joyce wasn't sure how long she'd been asleep before Vee shook her awake.

"Joycie, Joycie, wake up!" She looked at Vee through her sleepy half-closed eyes.

"What is it?"

"Freddy's wet himself again."

"Is he awake?"

"No. He's just lying in it."

"Leave it till morning, then. I don't want to have to wake him up."

Joyce's calm, reassuring voice wasn't enough for Vee who propped herself on one elbow and pulled as far away from her damp brother as the narrow shelter would allow. She turned up her nose and whined.

"But, Joyce . . . it's spread over to my bit!"

Joyce sighed heavily and ignored her.

"I can't sleep in it—it smells," Vee persisted.

Joyce, whispering as loud as she dared, quickly put an end to her sister's moaning.

"Oh, belt up, will you? You never stop whining, you're a pest. Go to sleep and shut up. You're a pain in the bum sometimes, Vee. Honest to God you are."

Grudgingly, Vee put her head down once more, closing her eyes but not to sleep. The sound they dreaded most, the siren, had started again. For the Harris kids it didn't just signal another raid, it was a ghoulish fanfare to a whole different adventure that would change their lives in the war, and perhaps for ever.

The bombs were very loud. As loud as they'd ever been. As loud as when they dropped on Dorkin Street and left a macabre playground of bombed ruins out of the bricks and rafters that once were people's homes.

Joyce was frightened, Vee could see it in her face. The corrugated iron Anderson shelter began to shake and vibrate as it had never done before.

"It's like travelling on the tube," said Wib, in an attempt to lighten matters. But Joyce was in no mood for his jokes.

"Don't be silly, Wib, it's serious. I'm going to get Mrs Johnson upstairs." Joyce threw off her blanket and ducked out of the shelter. Vee shouted after her.

"Don't be too long, Joycie."

Joyce never heard her. The explosions were far too loud, bursting all around her and lighting up the sky, like day.

Pushing hard on the back door, she ran into the dark house and stopped at the foot of the stairs. Suddenly, a bomb came down and seemed to go off right outside the house. Joyce flinched as the front room window blew in with an enormous crash of glass. She shouted up the narrow stairs.

"Mrs Johnson, are you there? It's me, Joycie. Mrs Johnson!" She shouted louder. "Are you there, Mrs Johnson, only we're scared. Can you come and sit with us till the raid's over? Please, Mrs Johnson, are you there? Please say you're there."

Instead of an answer, all she heard was the sound of another explosion that blew the coats off the hall-stand and Joyce off her feet. She lay there frightened to speak or move. Weakly, she called once more for Mrs Johnson but, by now, she knew she wasn't there. For a whole week the old lady had threatened to take refuge in the safety of the Underground, and tonight she'd obviously gone.

Joyce ran back down the garden and into the shelter. She didn't stop to look up into the sky above her, it was too frightening—like a firework night on November 5th that had gone hideously wrong.

Inside the shelter everyone was awake, even Siddy. He didn't quite understand what was happening, but the looks on his brothers' and sisters' faces were enough to scare him. Vee was the first to speak.

"What shall we do, Joycie? Where's Mrs Johnson?"

"She's not here, she's gone down the tube."

"What are we going to do then, Joycie?" Wib tried not to sound scared, but there was a choked-up, frightened frog in his throat that he couldn't disguise. He faked a cough to hide it.

Freddy stroked Darkie's shivering back as the poor dog whimpered, not understanding the horrible noises all around him.

Then came the loudest explosion so far. It was as if the German airmen had been given a map of Paxton Street as their special target. The bomb hit Mrs Huckle's grocer's shop on the corner of Paxton and Rochester Street. Fortunately Mrs Huckle had been evacuated to her sister's house in Pontypool, which was a god-send because the blast tore the tiny shop apart. The three houses either side of it also collapsed, as easily as a row of Vee and Joyce's dominoes.

It was all too much for Darkie. He suddenly jumped out from under Freddy's protective arms and scooted into the open. He yelped and barked, running back and forth in a confused frenzy that was half instinct and half plain fear. Joyce tried to grab Freddy as he dashed after Darkie, but he slipped through her hands.

"Freddy, Freddy, come here! Stay in the shelter, you bloody fool."

Darkie was totally confused. Around Paxton Street the glow of the fires made everything bright and Freddy could see the face of his dog quite clearly. The animal's eyes were filled with a terrible fear that Freddy couldn't begin to explain, because he didn't understand it either. Freddy grabbed his collar to hold him still and stroked his head to stop him trembling.

At that moment Joyce crawled out from the shelter and yanked hold of Freddy by the cardigan, forcing him to let go of Darkie's collar. The frightened dog leapt for the far wall and scrambled over it.

"Leave me alone, Joycie." Freddy was angry with Joyce. "I've got to get Darkie. You've let him go."

"You've got to get back in the shelter!"

"I've got to get Darkie!" Freddy struggled with his sister. She gripped even harder on to his cardigan but he'd lost sight of the dog and his anger gave him even more strength. The elbows of his cardigan ripped away at the seams as he pulled himself free. Joyce screamed at him as he scaled the wall in pursuit of Darkie. The sky burst into flames once more. It seemed that the bombs were getting nearer and nearer.

"Come back, Freddy, you bloody fool! Leave the dog. I'll tell Mum. You must get back in the shelter, Freddy! You'll get killed! Freddy! Freddy!"

Then Wib appeared from the shelter and, before Joyce could stop him, he too was up the wall and over the top. Joyce was beside herself with worry. It wasn't any fun being the eldest.

"Wib, not you too! Come ba-a-a-ck." She screamed at him, but it was no use, he'd gone in search of his brother.

Wib couldn't believe his eyes when he saw what the bombs had done to Paxton Street. The blast had left a hole in the middle of the road big enough to swallow up a double-decker bus. It had also swallowed up the hop-scotch and ripped the entire front wall off the tiny terraced houses. The gaping remains looked odd, with beds and sideboards poking out, plainly visible—almost as if the fronts had been opened up like giant dolls houses. Mr Palermo's lock-up had been flattened and a milky river of ice cream trickled along the pavement.

Freddy caught sight of Darkie's black tail vanishing behind the sandbags outside the fish shop. However, Mrs Saunders' sharp-pointed garden fence proved to be more awkward for a ten year old boy to climb than a frightened, bewildered dog. With great difficulty Freddy managed to struggle over, but it slowed him down long enough for Wib to catch him up.

"Freddy, don't be daft. You'll never catch

him. Let him go. We'll fetch him in the morning. We must go back inside the shelter. We'll get killed."

Freddy was in no mood to listen and even Wib's strong grip on his hair wasn't enough to deter him. He tugged away from Wib, who was left clutching a tuft of Freddy's locks.

As Freddy rushed across the street towards the fish shop, another bomb dropped. It was in the next street, but the blast was enough to knock Freddy off his feet and into a crater left by an earlier bomb. Wib was a little luckier. There was a large coping wall between him and the blast and apart from a gush of black soot that made him cough, he was unhurt. He dashed across to where Freddy had disappeared. Clambering down the sides of the hole, he tip-toed across a wooden rafter that had been thrown there from miles away. At the bottom of the hole Freddy was picking himself up, so Wib knew he couldn't be that badly hurt.

"You all right?" said Wib as he reached him.

"What?"

"Are you all right?"

"I can't hear you," Freddy replied.

Wib noticed there was blood trickling down the back of Freddy's neck. Hooking his arm around his brother's waist, he managed to drag him to the top of the hole and across the street, back to the safety of the garden shelter.

Joyce wrapped a blanket around Freddy's shoulders, and the rest of them, Siddy, Vee and Wib, just sat and stared at him, not sure what to say or do. Shocked and dazed, his pale face looked even paler than normal. Especially in contrast to Wib, whose sooty appearance made him look like a coalman. Freddy cupped his hands over his ears and screwed up his face. He was obviously in great pain.

"My ears hurt me."

"Can you hear all right?" said Joyce.

"Just," said Freddy. "All I can hear is whistling sounds, like a train whistle."

"But can you hear us?" Wib persisted where Joyce left off.

"Very faintly, but mostly it's just a whistle."

No one spoke. They just looked at Freddy.

"I think it's a bit better," he said, taking his hands away from his ears.

"Can you hear us now?" said Joyce.

Freddy nodded.

"It's O.K. Only I've got a headache."

"Haven't we all," said Wib, relieved that his brother was back to normal. Joyce rolled her eyes upwards and let out a sigh of relief.

"We'll have to stay here for the time being. Vee, throw me that extra blanket for Siddy."

Joyce wrapped her arms around Siddy and Vee. Freddy and Wib snuggled even closer together as the five of them lay there in silence.

The candle flame flickered precariously in the draught but, thankfully, never blew out. Its warm glow was their only comfort.

As the sounds of the bombs began to die down, Joyce spoke.

"Are you all right, you lot?"

Wib was the only one to answer. "I'd sooner be on my holidays."

Vee and Joyce laughed out loud at Wib's silly joke. Somehow it was easier than crying.

CHAPTER 3
A WHISTLE IN THE EARS

Joyce dared not look outside the door of the Anderson shelter. The continuous wail of the all-clear siren said the raid was over and the bombers had gone for the time being.

Outside, the ear-splitting sounds of explosions and ack-ack shells had briefly given way to silence, which was promptly ended by the bell-clanging of fire engines and the urgent shouts of A.R.P. men and other rescue workers.

Wib had collected his picture cards together into the Player's tin and tucked it away inside his cardigan. The shelter was hot and stuffy and very different from the chill of previous nights. Smoke and dust from the burning debris outside drifted in, making Siddy's eyes water and tickling Vee's nose so that she began to sneeze repeatedly.

"Bless you," said Joyce each time.

"Do you think we should put our gas-masks on, Joycie?" Vee asked, sneezing once more.

"It's smoke not gas, you daft 'appath," said Wib.

"How do you know it's not gas? *Atishoo!*"

"'Cause you'd have heard the sound of the rattles."

"Who told you?"

"Mr Cadwaller. That's where he got his cough from. He got gassed in the trenches in the last war. Read your leaflet, it's all in there."

Wib pointed to the neat pile of cardboard boxes that contained the precious gas-masks. Siddy started to cough and rub his eyes. Joyce pulled his hand away.

"Don't do that, you'll make it worse." She tried to pretend it was all right but the smoke was getting thicker. It hung in a cloud, visible to all in the candle-light. Wib spoke up.

"Shall I see if it's all right outside now, Joycie?"

"No. Stay where you are. Mum said if anything should happen to stay put."

"How long for?" Freddy asked. "We could be here for days and they'd never know." He opened his mouth wide and tugged at his ear lobe to stop the whistling in his head.

Wib propped himself on one hand and fiddled with the wax on the candle as it dripped on to the saucer. He yawned as he spoke.

"I read about a man who could sniff out dead bodies under all the rubble."

"We're not dead though, are we?" said Freddy.

"I know we're not."

"So why go on about dead bodies then, stupid," Vee chimed in.

"Because I never read about a man who sniffed out *live* people, that's why."

Suddenly all their questions were answered. They heard the sound they had been listening for ever since the raid had begun: their mother's voice.

"Joycie! Are you in there? Are you all right? Joycie?"

Joyce eagerly shouted her reply.

"Yes. We're all right, Mum. Except Freddy's hurt his ears."

The curtain hanging at the shelter entrance was pulled across, revealing not their mother but an air-raid warden whose white hat and red face were black with soot.

"Out you come, my sunshines, everything's all right. Your mum's here."

The warden emerged from the shelter carrying Siddy, and Mrs Harris took him in her arms. One by one the children climbed out and clutched their mother good and hard. Vi Harris didn't say anything and neither did the kids. They were so pleased to see her, words just weren't needed. Freddy forgot the whistling in his ears for a moment and looked around for Darkie, but there didn't seem to be any sign of him.

Joyce, Vee and Wib stared up at their house, or what was left of it. Like the houses either side, there was a large gaping hole in the front and the roof had collapsed, taking most of the top floor with it.

Vee noticed that their bed had dropped a whole floor and now stood precariously on its end on top of the kitchen stove.

"Good job we weren't sleeping in it," she said.

"Now Mum can cook the dinner without getting out of bed," Wib quipped.

Joyce gave him a sharp push in the back.

"Be quiet, Wib. It's not funny."

In the corner of the garden, out of earshot of the children, Mrs Harris was in urgent conversation with the air-raid warden. She was pointing at the house and seemed to be growing more and more upset. Siddy was shifted from one tired arm to the other. The warden just kept shaking his head, and the more he did so the more it upset Mrs Harris. It was plain to see that no one could live in the bombed-out house, but Vi Harris wasn't going to leave it in a hurry. Vee and Wib sat down on the upturned tin bath that had been blasted off the garden wall.

Another friendly warden wrapped a thick white bandage around Freddy's head. The young invalid smiled. It made him feel quite important to get all this attention. Wib watched, a little envious that he too couldn't look like a proper casualty. Freddy suddenly winced as the warden touched his ear.

"Ooh, be careful, mister."

The warden pressed gently around the ear

once more.

"Does that hurt you, son?"

"A bit—it makes my ears whistle."

"He got caught in the street by a blast," said Wib.

Joyce squeezed his arm to shut him up, but Mrs Harris had heard.

"What was he doing out in the street, Joycie? I told you never to leave the shelter."

"He was chasing Darkie, Mum. I told him not to, honest I did. He wouldn't listen. Darkie ran out and he ran after him."

"It wasn't her fault, Mum." Wib and Vee spoke up for their sister.

"He ran after Darkie. Stupid he was. We told him not to."

The warden interrupted them.

"Well, he'll have to go to hospital, love, just to be on the safe side. Get his ears checked. You can't be too careful. Funny things ears."

The warden in the once white hat handed mugs of hot tea to Vee and Joyce.

"There you are, darling, share that amongst you." He handed another mug to Mrs Harris who quietened down considerably after sipping the steaming brown liquid. The warden spoke to her in a soft whisper.

"I suggest you take this lot to the communal shelter down at Mannix Street for the rest of the night. We'll pop the lad into you after he's been to the hospital.''

Mrs Harris nodded agreement and finished her tea. She pulled a face as she swallowed the tea leaves by mistake.

''Come on, loves. We're off. Freddy lovey, you're going with this nice man to the hospital.''

''What for? It's only a headache, honestly.'' Freddy wasn't pleased at the prospect of being on his own.

''Don't worry, love, it's only for half an hour. Take 'em five minutes to look at your ears and give you something for your headache.''

Freddy wasn't convinced but allowed the warden to lead him away.

''What about our things, Mum?'' Joyce was concerned at leaving their prized possessions, however few, in the wide-open house.

''Better to come back for your bits and pieces tomorrow, love,'' the warden chipped in. ''It's not safe to go in now.''

The two wardens helped Mrs Harris and the children over the back wall. The barrage balloons were lit up by the search-lights that swept across the black sky, looking for straggling enemy bombers. It seemed to be quiet—for a while at least.

The large red and white sign on the side of the brick building at the end of Mannix Street said ''Shelter for 80 Persons'', and a large red arrow pointed the way to the concealed entrance.

Inside, the sign had been blatantly ignored

because nearly 200 people had sheltered there. Normally the shelter warden would have turfed out any extra visitors, but with the bombs as bad as they were, regulations and red and white official notices were conveniently overlooked.

Vi Harris pushed her children into a narrow gap in between two wooden bunks that were occupied by the regular shelterers.

On one side was a family of rather comical looking ginger-haired people. The mother of the family sat on the top bunk like an enormous chicken, handing out mugs of tea and jam sandwiches to her red-haired youngsters. In a coarse cockney voice she bleated, "Get that down you, Elsie—get that down you, Arthur—get that down you, Derek."

In contrast, the family on the other side of them couldn't be seen; just half-a-dozen lumps snoring away under the warm blankets. Vi Harris and the kids made themselves as comfortable as they could. Siddy looked the most miserable and his sad face was spotted by the gentleman whose head poked out from the blanket on the bottom bunk next to him. The man wore a warm balaclava helmet. He made a clicking noise with his teeth to get Siddy's attention. Siddy yawned and rubbed his nose before looking at the man out of the corner of his eye. It was a good job he did. From under the grey blanket the man took out a half-eaten bar of Fry's chocolate. He snapped off a tiny, but delicious-looking square and handed it to Siddy, who snatched it rather rudely. Wib watched the proceedings with great interest, licking his lips as Siddy popped the chocolate into his mouth. Never one to miss an opportunity, Wib spoke up.

''Er, I don't suppose there's a chance of another bit where that came from, is there, guv?'' Mr Balaclava Helmet grumbled under his breath and offered another square of chocolate to Wib, who winked to show his gratitude.

On the other side of him Vee and Joyce had snuggled up together and drifted into sleep. Wib, sucking the last of the chocolate from the inside of his mouth, looked towards Siddy.

''Nice?''

Siddy nodded in agreement. It certainly was. Quite possibly the best they'd ever tasted.

CHAPTER 4
TIMBER SKELETONS

The trouble with shelters was that you never knew when it was morning. There were no windows, and the curtain of sacking material in front of the entrance ensured that all the electric light was kept in and the daylight out.

The red-haired family were the first awake. The father was a tall, lanky man with a zig-zag patterned woolly and baggy bloodshot eyes that matched his shock of red hair. It is not unfair to say he looked like a dressed-up carrot.

Siddy was the first of the Harris family to wake up. Hands in pockets, he casually walked the length of the shelter, looking up and down the rows of wooden bunks. He stopped at a bunk where a plump lady, surrounded by half-a-dozen bundles, twirled her dry, unwashed hair into rather vicious-looking metal curlers. This intrigued Siddy no end and he stood and stared just long enough to receive a Garibaldi biscuit and a "shoo" on his way.

Mrs Harris shook the rest of the children awake. Wib looked around for Freddy but there was no sign of him.

"Where's Freddy, Mum?" he said, yawning so widely you could see his tonsils.

"He's still at the hospital. They kept him in."

"How do you know that?" queried Wib.

"'Cause someone told me."

"Who?"

"The warden."

"When? I didn't see no warden."

"When you were asleep. Stop asking questions, Wib, and get yourself ready. We're going. Pick up your gas-masks."

Wib was annoyed with himself for falling asleep and missing something.

"Where we going, Mum?" asked Joyce.

"Where do you think? Home of course . . . and then to the hospital to fetch Freddy."

Joyce and Vee were a little puzzled at the remark. They'd seen with their own eyes that their house had been damaged beyond repair—but their mother hadn't seemed to notice. Nevertheless, the four of them followed her towards the exit door. They stopped briefly to look at a man who was stripped to the waist and washing in a red metal fire-bucket. The sight of the cold water made them shiver.

"Want a wash, son?" the man said to Wib, who looked with horror at the icy-cold water.

"No thanks, mister. I'm allergic to water. It brings me out in spots."

The hard sunlight made them blink as they stepped out of the shelter and Mrs Harris set a brisk pace as she led them off down Mannix Street.

The dreadful results of the previous night's raid were everywhere to be seen. There were scores of homeless people, in small groups, wandering in a dozen different directions, clutching their belongings or pushing prams piled high with bundles and salvaged furniture.

Soldiers in long leather waistcoats pulled down unsafe walls, the remnants of bombed-out houses. Wib smiled at a dirty-faced fireman who rolled up his hose with arms weary from a night of fire-fighting.

Mrs Harris led the children on a detour around a burst water main that had left an enormous puddle across the road. Wib splashed through it, much to the disapproval of Mrs Harris.

"Don't do that, Wib, you silly boy. You'll get your socks wet."

"Sorry, Mum."

It seemed that every street they went down had been caught by the bombs. The side alleys and short cuts were blocked by piles of bricks and splintered roof timbers. Familiar shops had been turned into unfamiliar blackened, empty shells. Vee noticed a broken scooter sticking out from a pile of rubble.

"Joycie. D'you think the swing gardens got bombed?"

Joyce shrugged her shoulders. The water in Wib's plimsolls made a loud squelching noise as he ran up behind them.

"With any luck they bombed the school as

well. They send you home if your school gets bombed. That's what happened at St. Mary's, the kids didn't have to go to school for weeks."

In the High Street they noticed that Mr Palermo had changed his name to Palmer. In big white letters, over his ice cream shop, he'd painted "BRITISH SUBJECT". The window was also smashed, whether by a bomb or by someone who didn't like Italians, they never knew.

They turned the corner by "Bestworks Boot and Shoe Repairers". Across the window it normally said, "Save your sole for 1/6d", in beautiful maroon and gold lettering. But now it was just an empty space with dozens of boots and shoes spread across the pavement, amongst the shattered pieces of the old window.

But it wasn't Bestworks that everyone was looking at. Wib gulped as he saw what had happened to the rest of Paxton Street.

"Where's the houses gone?"

The whole of the street had been gutted by fire. The blasted houses they had left behind were now just a row of charred timber skeletons, silhouetted against the cloudless sky.

"Where we going to live now, Joycie?" whispered Vee.

"Ssh! What shall we do, Mum?" Joyce spoke up for the rest of them.

Mrs Harris hadn't said a word. She too was in a state of shock and didn't quite know where to turn.

"I don't know. I really don't know, Joycie."

Just then an A.R.P. warden emerged from Bestworks with a clipboard. He had a dull, monotonous voice that people with clipboards often have.

"You live in this street, love?"

"Yes."

"Which one?"

"Number eight, over there."

Mrs Harris pointed to the pathetic smoking remains.

"Name?"

"Harris."

"Number in family?"

"Six. Well—five now 'cause one's in hospital."

"Right, love. Larkwood Street School Reception Centre is where you've got to go to—they'll soon fix you up, not to worry."

There was absolutely no emotion in his flat official's voice. But strangely, it was reassuring. And his smile made them smile.

"I'll go there now. Can I drop this lot off at school?"

"Which school?"

"William Ockforth," answered the children in unison. It used to be called Buxley Street School before someone at the council had the bright idea to change the name. Who William Ockforth was no one knew—except, of course, he was something to do with the council.

The warden shook his head.

"No luck there, I'm afraid. It caught one as well. Incendiaries everywhere last night. My advice to you is to get down to Larkwood straight away and get yourself enrolled. They'll sort you out in no time."

Mrs Harris turned away from Paxton Street and the four children plodded after her.

It seemed funny having no house, no belongings and now, not even a school to go to. But, curiously, it was difficult to be sad. Wib clutched his tin of picture cards and whistled his favourite tune, "Umbrella Man", as he brought up the rear of the small group.

Somehow, as they walked away from the sad remains of their old house, it seemed like they were walking away from an old world and into a new one. The prospect made Wib whistle even louder.

CHAPTER 5
AUNTIE DOLLY

The official-looking sign on the wall at Larkwood School said: "Meat Dish 4d; Afters 2d; Tea 1d; Children's Portions half-price", and in even larger letters underneath: "ABSOLUTELY NO SECOND PORTIONS. THERE'S A WAR ON."

Joyce handed in the family's free meal tickets that they had collected downstairs in the hall. Back across the wooden trestle table came five deep, white enamel plates, filled to the brim with a bubbling hot stew. Great chunks of meat and potatoes slopped about in the brown gravy; Wib's mouth watered at the delicious sight. There was also a large plate of bread and margarine. Mrs Harris arrived, clutching a handful of official leaflets and forms. She filled them in whilst the children tucked into their stew.

"What's the game then, Mum?" said Wib, briefly looking up from his food. Mrs Harris didn't answer. She tucked her hair behind her ears and shook her head, indicating that she didn't want to be bothered.

Wib flicked over one of the official pamphlets on the table and read it aloud.

"After the raid. Keep this and do what it tells you. Help is waiting for you. The Government, your fellow citizens and your neighbours will see that the 'Front Line Fighters' are looked after."

Wib quite liked the idea of being a 'Front Line Fighter'. Especially if you got free stew. Mrs Harris looked up from the last of her forms.

"Right. That's it. Now here's what I want you to do, Joycie. You're to take Wib and Vee to your Auntie Dolly's. I'm taking Siddy to the hospital with me to fetch Freddy.

"Aunty Dolly?" said Vee with some surprise. Auntie Dolly was her mother's half-sister and they rarely saw one another. On the occasions that they did, it would always end in an argument. In fact the children hadn't even met her. Mrs Harris continued her instructions to Joyce.

"Here's her address." She tore a corner off one of the pamphlets and scribbled something on it.

"You go over Canal Bridge and it's the third turning on the left before the gasworks. Tell her who you are and ask her to put you up for the night. I'll pop along and meet you when I've seen how Freddy is."

"Does she know we're coming, Mum?" Joyce had to ask, knowing how Auntie Dolly disliked them so.

"No, but tell her what's happened to our house and I'll explain the rest when I see her."

Mrs Harris swallowed a couple of mouthfuls of her own stew and pushed it away from her. Wib and Vee leaned across and with a couple of swift spoonfuls, finished it off.

"Right, off we go. First we've got to get some clothes." As if on cue, Siddy sneezed into his empty plate.

"Bless you," said Joyce and Vee together.

"What kind of clothes?" asked Wib, half expecting to be kitted out in a fireman's uniform.

"Warm clothes. You can't walk around the streets like you are, can you? You'll catch your death of cold."

The family filed out of the emergency canteen. As they passed the trestle table, Wib noticed that a gust of wind from the door had blown some free meal tickets on to the floor. He stopped briefly, under the pretence of doing up his shoe-lace, and quickly slipped a handful into his pocket. They would come in handy. After all, as things were going, he never knew when they might need them.

Mrs Harris pushed them inside the room marked "BOMB VICTIMS. CLOTHING." Vee didn't like being a 'victim'. Neither did she like the look of the enormous pile of 'generously donated' second-hand clothes.

Everything they tried on seemed to be three sizes too big, and Joyce and Wib began to giggle at the long arms and baggy sleeves of their ill-fitting coats.

"Don't be rude, you lot," said Mrs Harris. She turned to the W.V.S. lady who handed out the clothes.

"They don't mean to be cheeky, ma'am.

They're ever so grateful, really."

Vee didn't look very grateful. She wasn't keen on her hat and coat at all. The funny stiff collar made her neck itch and the brown beret gave her the appearance of a chocolate lollypop. She preferred her own coat, left behind in the bombing. True it had holes in the elbows but she'd grown quite attached to it.

The W.V.S. lady pulled out a couple of hats from the pile of clothing and handed them to Mrs Harris. Wib was very complimentary.

"It looks lovely, Mum, really nice."

Compliments or not, Mrs Harris tried on another hat which she liked better. Wib was undeterred.

"That looks lovely, Mum, even nicer."

Mrs Harris smiled at the W.V.S. lady.

"Thank you very much, love. What do you say, kids?"

"Thank you very much, miss."

Vee wasn't so thankful. She said nothing as she walked out the door. She still preferred her own coat. Holes in the elbows or not.

Auntie Dolly's house was through a narrow alley at the back of a coal shop. "Back of Beechams" was all Mrs Harris had written down; Joyce checked the piece of paper with the name at the top of the shop: "Beechams Best Nuts".

"I think this is it," she said.

Slowly, ever so slowly, they tip-toed into the dark, cavernous interior of the shop. There was coal piled either side like two enormous indoor slag-heaps. A glow of yellow light was coming from the rear of the shop and they could hear a continual scraping noise. Joyce and Vee turned the corner.

"Yes? How much do you want?" The loud bellowing voice came from a short, grey-haired lady with flabby, blotchy pink arms. She vigorously shovelled coal into a metal scoop, which hung by chains on one side of an enormous pair of scales.

"We don't want any coal, lady, we're looking for our Auntie Dolly," said Joyce.

"Dolly? Up there," said the stout lady, pulling up her black apron and pointing up some stone steps with her elbow.

"Mind yourself on the stairs—bit steep those stairs." She carried on shovelling the coal, almost as if the three children weren't there.

There was no hand-rail to the stone steps and they twisted awkwardly and steeply upwards. At the top was a soot-covered door, which made Joyce's hands dirty just touching the knocker. Vee and Wib looked down at the old lady who was still bagging up the coal.

Auntie Dolly's door was opened by a small girl, whose snotty nose was in urgent need of a handkerchief. Joyce bent down to talk to her.

"Could you get your mum, please?"

The three Harris children waited while the girl scampered down the hall; a nasty, dirty-looking area which seemed to be even blacker than the coal-yard downstairs.

Auntie Dolly appeared from the scullery at the back. She was a scruffy woman with a hard, craggy face and sad, deep-sunken eyes. If you really looked hard you could see a slight resemblance between her and Mrs Harris, but only just. To Joyce, Vee and Wib, she was a total stranger.

"Yes? What do you want?"

She wiped her hands on a tea towel as she spoke.

"Er, Auntie Dolly? Our Mum's your sister Vi. This is Vee and Wib. I'm Joyce. Mum sent us."

"Sent you here? Why?"

"Because, you see, we got bombed out last night and our house is burned down and Mum wondered if you could put us up . . ."

"Put you up?"

"For the night."

"The three of you?" Auntie Dolly's voice wasn't the friendliest they'd come across. All the stories Joyce had heard about the two half-sisters came flooding back. Horrible stories of screaming fights, hair pulling and neighbours calling the police. Joyce carried on, trying to ignore the coldness in her aunt's voice.

"Well there's three of us now, but Mum's coming on later with Siddy; he's our little brother and if Freddy's ears are better he's coming too. He's our other brother—and Wibby's twin, only he don't look like him."

"You're joking. I can't take you lot. I've got my in-laws staying with me—they got bombed out last week. I've no more room. I've got three kids of me own as well, remember. Your mother had no business sending you here."

Joyce wasn't quite sure what to do. Her last instructions from her mother were to go and stay at Auntie Dolly's, yet the very same lady wasn't even letting her in the door. Wib on the other hand was quite pleased. He didn't like what he saw in Auntie Dolly's hall and as far as Auntie Dolly herself was concerned, he would be more than pleased *not* to make her acquaintance.

"Sorry, but it's impossible . . . it's not that I don't want to. There's just not enough room, see? Honest, I'd take you if I could. But I'm not a magician, am I? There's just no room."

She was a terrible liar because her eyes gave her away. Joyce nodded and beckoned the others to follow her down the stone steps.

"Thank you. Bye."

"Bye," said Vee and Wib with as much politeness as they could muster. They walked past the stout lady in the black apron and out into the daylight.

Joyce was a little puzzled as to what to do next. Vee tucked her skirt into her knickers and did a hand-stand against the wall. Wib climbed up a lamp-post and swung from the metal ladder-rest at the top. He dropped to the pavement; his thin-soled plimsolls were not much protection and the landing stung the bottoms of his feet.

"Right," said Joyce, making up her mind. "There's no point in hanging around here. We'll have to go and find Mum."

"Where though, Joycie?"

"At the hospital."

"Which hospital?"

"I don't know, we'll have to try 'em all. We'll start at the Hackney General."

As the three of them skipped down the alley they were watched by Auntie Dolly's little girl, who pressed her face up against the window. Her nose was still in need of a handkerchief, which she didn't have, so she made do with the curtain.

CHAPTER 6
LOST

Apart from the burst water main, which still flooded across the road, the High Street was more or less back to normal. Everywhere people swept up broken glass and cleared away awkward piles of rubble. There were "Business As Usual" signs in every window, including Mr Palermo's ice cream shop, which was untrue because even Wib knew he had none.

Joyce led Wib and Vee along the street, passing familiar shops that they'd known all their lives. Past Beckie's Bag Wash and Willcock's English Hairdressers, where you could get a proper haircut for fourpence and a rather severe "all-off" for threeepence. Past Rosie Long's Rag Shop, which for some strange reason sold cat's meat, the smell of which could be experienced two streets away. Past Granny Elliott's Sweet Shop where you could get a glass thimble of Tizer—"The Appetizer"—for a penny, and for a farthing you could buy an "everlasting stick" of "Spanish wood" that you could chew on for ages. They never knew it then, but they were passing these familiar shops for the last time.

Over Canal Bridge, Wib spotted a section of soldiers who were hurrying along the tow-path by Eagle Wharf, at the double. Before the war the canal tow-path had been Wib and Freddy's secret playground, but now it was forbidden to anyone who didn't wear an official's arm-band.

Joyce ran up the stairs of the Hackney General Hospital, closely followed by the other two. An enormous wall of sandbags protected the front entrance and they threaded their way through a small maze to get to the porter's cubby-hole. Joyce poked her head through the open window.

"Excuse me, sir. Do you have a Freddy Harris in here?"

"Harris? When did he come in?"

"Last night."

"First name?"

"Freddy . . . er, Frederick . . . he's got bad ears."

The porter ran his finger down a long line of names, but was unable to find Freddy Harris.

"Hockstead, Hickney, Horry, Hutchinson . . . but no Harris. Sorry, love, no Harris here . . ."

Joyce repeated her request.

"Harris. Freddy Harris. You sure he's not there? You don't know where else he could be, do you?"

The porter lifted up his cap and scratched a very sweaty bald head.

"Try Lotts Lane Infirmary. They might have him. They've got a lot of bomb casualties."

"Thank you. We'll try there."

Lotts Lane had no F. Harris registered, either.

Nor did Portchurch Street or Gaston Road Casualty, and, worse still, Larkin Street Reception Centre had no record of Freddy, let alone news of Mum and Siddy. The severity of the previous night's raid had thrown the already tired staff at the centre into greater confusion than ever. Joyce had asked so many people and checked so many lists, she was beginning to despair. Everyone was polite but everyone seemed to pass her on to someone else. Joyce and Vee put down their gas-mask cases and sat by the sand-bagged police telephone box, outside the school gates. Wib kneeled down on the kerb and absent-mindedly scratched the dirt out of the cracks in the gutter. None of them were quite sure what to do next.

"I think we should go to a police station, Joycie," said Wib, "else we could be walking the streets all night. And that won't be too clever once the raids start."

Joyce looked up at the sky. She too had thought about the possibility of an air-raid, and in an hour or so it would be dark. The thought made her button up her coat and drag herself to her feet.

"Right. Who wants a cup of tea and a saveloy?"

The very idea of a juicy red saveloy made Vee and Wib spring to their feet. Just then, Wib noticed an old Morris shooting-brake stop at the corner. It was driven by a special constable and in the back Wib could see a dozen or so dogs, quietly staring out of the back windows.

"Look, Joycie, dogs!" Vee and Wib ran across

the road towards the old Morris. There were all sorts of stray dogs, mostly mongrels, but there was no sign of Darkie.

"You haven't seen a black dog with a white bit on his face, have you, mister?" Vee asked the constable in the driving cab.

"Love, I've seen every sort of dog imaginable in the last few weeks. Black ones, brown ones, ginger ones. You name it, I've seen it. You'll have to check with your local A.R.P. man—he'll have a record."

"O.K. Thank you," said Vee. Some hopes, she thought. So far today they'd managed to lose their mum and two little brothers, so there wasn't much chance of finding a stray dog.

Mrs Grabowski, who had the saveloy shop in Laycock Street, was always a soft touch for Wib. "Her cheeky little monkey," she called him. Wib even put up with her squeezing his cheek, because if he hung around long enough she always slipped him an extra saveloy. True, in war-time, they had more bread in them than meat, but it was welcome just the same.

Joyce and Vee walked down Laycock Street, eating their saveloys. As they turned the corner, the welcome sight of a W.V.S. "free-tea" wagon made them lengthen their stride. There was the usual queue of homeless people. The children waited their turn, until three hot cups of tea were pushed across the counter towards them. Joyce sat down on the window-sill of a bombed house. Should they go back to Auntie Dolly's? After all, that's where their mum had told them to go. Maybe she had persuaded her to let them stay. They should have stayed outside the coal shop and waited. Joyce stamped her foot on the pavement, annoyed at herself for wasting time walking the streets. Now she had decided.

"Right. We'll have to go back to Auntie Dolly's."

"Oh, no," said Wib, "not that horrible hole."

"Mum said to go there and that's where we should have stayed."

Joyce picked up her gas-mask and walked off down the cobbled street. Wib didn't even have time to finish his tea. He was beginning to get a bit fed up with being lost.

The old lady in the black apron was putting up the shutters outside the coal shop when the children arrived. Joyce ran up the stone steps to Auntie Dolly's door.

"They're not in, love. You're wasting your time. They're all down the tube. After last night I think half the street's down there."

"Did our mum come here, lady? Did you see her? She had two boys with her."

"Yeah, I saw her. But only one little nipper she had with her."

"Where did she go? She didn't tell you where she went, did she?"

"Search me. Down the tube as well, I s'pose. She hung about here for ages waiting for you."

"Which tube?"

The coal lady shrugged her big shoulders. "God knows. I hide under the stairs, myself. You wouldn't get me down no tube. Too close to other people for my liking."

Joyce thanked her and dashed out into the street, closely followed by Wib and Vee.

"Which tube station we going to then, Joycie?"

"The nearest."

"How do we know what's the nearest?"

"We don't."

"We might be going in the wrong direction."

"We ask someone."

At the corner of the street two young soldiers were busily filling sandbags. Joyce headed straight for them.

"Excuse me, could you tell me where the nearest underground station is, please?"

"Mile End or Bethnal Green, love. They're about the same—or as near as makes no difference."

Joyce had to make a quick decision.

"Which one is this way?"

The soldier pointed with his shovel.

"Mile End. Down this road here till you get to the bottom, turn left across the park, keep going. You'll see it at the bottom of Grove Road. O.K.? If you get lost, ask someone else."

Before the young soldier had finished giving his directions, Joyce heard the noise she'd been dreading; the sound of the siren. The soldier looked up towards the sky. It was a natural reaction.

"They're early tonight. You'd better get a move on, kids."

Joyce, Vee and Wib didn't need any telling. They were already running.

CHAPTER 7
DOWN THE TUBE

The guns in Victoria Park had already opened fire as Joyce, Vee and Wib passed. The loud explosions made them run even faster. Vee's gas-mask case bobbed up and down awkwardly as she rushed along.

The wintry evening light was beginning to dim and the black-out would mean no street lights to guide them. Joyce knew they had to reach the station before dark. The pace was too fast for Wib's liking. His two sisters were always better runners than he was and he was beginning to get a stitch. Clutching his side, he yelled at his elder sister.

"Joycie! Can you stop a bit, please. I've got a stitch!"

Joyce looked back but didn't stop running.

"We can't stop now, Wib, can you hold out till we get to the station?"

Wib didn't answer, but he stopped anyway and leaned against a boarded-up shop window.

"Wib! Come on!" Joyce shouted at her red-faced brother.

"I've got to have a breather, Joycie! Just a little one, else I'll pass out, honest I will."

At that moment there was an enormous

explosion from the other side of Victoria Park. It was a long way from them but it was close enough to set Wib running again. By now there were other people running along the pavement and, to Wib, they all seemed to be moving faster than he was—like in a bad dream when you run and run and never seem to get anywhere. Even a man on crutches overtook him—and he only had one leg!

Joyce stopped briefly by the wall of sandbags that surrounded the post office. Her lungs were starting to ache with all the running, but she couldn't let the other two know. Vee was the best runner in her class and hardly seemed out of breath. Wib arrived last. He was in a terrible state and could hardly speak, which was unusual for him.

"I've got spots in front of my eyes," he panted. "I think I'm going to die."

"Don't be stupid," said Joyce, "it's not far now."

"How far?" Wib was certainly no athlete and normally his picture cards were the nearest he ever got to a sporting activity.

"I can see it from here," Joyce fibbed, because she couldn't see a thing.

"Bloody silly coat," muttered Vee, as she folded back the over-long sleeves.

"Don't swear, Vee."

"I think I'm going to be sick, Joycie," said Wib, clamping his hand over his face.

At that moment another bomb dropped

ahead of them, throwing great orange flames into the sky and silhouetting the dome of the Odeon cinema so it looked like a black cardboard cut-out. Needless to say, Wib started running again. Joyce didn't have to pretend any more; through the smoky evening light, she could see queues of people filing down the stairs into the Underground. Special constables and A.R.P. men barked out orders to encourage the crowd not to rush or panic. Mostly people were quite orderly, but the pounding of the ack-ack shells and the exploding bombs quickened everybody's pace.

Joyce grabbed Wib's hand as she joined the crowd jogging down the stairs. Normally, Wib didn't like holding girls' hands—but as the crush grew, he clung on hard so as not to lose his sister. To her horror, Vee found she was getting left behind. She shouted over the head of the woman in front of her.

"Joycie, wait a minute! You're going too fast for me."

"Don't worry! We'll wait for you at the bottom of the stairs."

Vee clutched her gas-mask and let herself be carried along by the crowd. It was a funny sensation, walking almost without your feet touching the ground.

At the bottom of the stairs, along the winding cream-tiled tunnels, things weren't quite so hectic. People had settled in for the night, wrapped in warm blankets and armed with thermos flasks of tea. There was even a man with an accordian and a monkey who was entertaining some miserable-looking children. Their long faces indicated that he wasn't having much luck.

There were literally hundreds of families piled together, right up to the edge of the platform. Wib looked down at the electric rails and wondered what would happen if someone toppled over in their sleep. Then the Harris children saw the sight they had been longing for all day. Sitting underneath a poster for Andrew's Liver Salts were Mum and Siddy.

Joyce shouted out as loud as she could.

"Mum. We're over here! Mum!"

Mrs Harris jumped to her feet and ran towards them, not really worrying who she trod on in the process.

"Watch it, you clumsy cow!" shouted a woman who had her hat knocked off.

Mrs Harris hugged her three children to her and kissed them over and over again. Wib was a little embarrassed at being kissed in front of so many people, but put up with it all the same. They made their way back through the crowds towards Siddy, who was smiling all over his face at the sight of his brother and sisters. Joyce started to explain, but it wasn't necessary.

"We went to Auntie Dolly's, Mum, but she wouldn't have us and then, when we went back, we'd missed you."

"Don't worry, love, you're here now. Not to worry."

They all sat down beneath the Andrew's poster, and each tried to get a question in first.

"Where's Freddy, Mum? Is he still in hospital?"

"Yes, he's got to stay in to have something done to his ears. It might take a while."

"How about Darkie? Any news?"

"No news, love. They say there's hundreds of dogs and cats wandering all over the place since the raids started."

"Where we going then, Mum?" asked Wib. "Where are we going to live?"

Mrs Harris made Siddy's head comfortable in her lap and put her arm around Vee, who leaned against her mother's chest.

"Well, I've thought about it a lot. Your Auntie Dolly won't have us so I've spoken to . . . er . . . Uncle Stanley."

Joyce and Wib's ears pricked up. Their mother had never really talked about him before.

". . . I've spoken to Uncle Stanley and he's not got a lot of room above the pub, it's only a small flat, you see . . ."

She gulped and pulled the wisp of hair out of Vee's eyes as she spoke.

". . . but he said he'll put us up."

Joyce smiled at the news, but not for long.

"What all of us?"

Mrs Harris looked down into her lap.

"Er, no. Not all of you. Just Siddy and me."

"But what about the rest of us? Where will we live?"

"I've thought about it a lot. The bombing's not getting any better. We've got no home that you can speak of. So I think it's best . . . safer at any rate . . ."

"What Mum?" Joyce urged her mother to finish.

"I've decided to have you evacuated."

The news stunned all three of them into silence. For a long time no one spoke. Not that any one could have heard them because at that moment a train thundered through the station. Wib and Vee looked at one another as the lights from the speeding train flickered across their faces.

Evacuation meant being sent away, maybe a long way, from London. It was a frightening thought. Up to now the furthest they'd ever been was a fourpenny bus ride.

CHAPTER 8
THE GOOD SHIP LOLLYPOP

Paddington Station was the biggest building Wib had ever seen. There were people everywhere; chatty children, tearful mums, grim-faced dads, bossy railway officials, frantic W.V.S. ladies, nurses, soldiers and policemen. All sorts. In fact, apart from the time his dad took him to see West Ham in the Cup, he'd never before seen so many people.

He sniffed the air and breathed in the unique oily, smoky railway smell which he found quite pleasant. Mrs Harris led the way through the crowds; judging by the lost, bewildered look on her face, she was as unused to railway stations as the rest of them. Wib was intrigued by three helmeted policemen who ferretted amongst some mailbags. He wondered what they were looking for.

Vee clutched her pillow-case. It was a funny thing to carry your clothes in, she thought. After all, she only had a spare vest, socks and knickers and an extra woolly, anyway. Wib had tied a piece of string around his pillow-case, which meant he could throw it over his shoulder like a pirate. Closing one eye he hopped along making jokes like, "Ah, me hearties, pieces of eight, shiver me timbers." If the truth be known, he wasn't very funny at all; but Vee and Joyce giggled at him anyway because everything seemed so exciting—not at all as miserable as they thought it was going to be.

Joyce squealed as a porter trod on her foot, making her drop her brown paper parcel.

"Ouch! Mind where you're going!"

"Sorry, love. Can't see a thing today, lost me specs in the black-out."

"It's O.K.," said Joyce, a little unconvincingly because she was sure, at the very least, he'd crushed her little toe through her thin canvas shoes. A soldier picked up her fallen bundle and handed it to her.

"Dropped your spare undies, love."

He winked at Joyce and her pale skin turned to deep scarlet when she noticed the parcel had torn open and her spare pair of white socks was hanging out.

"Come on, loves. Hurry up," shouted Mrs Harris. She was pleased she'd left Siddy at the Co-Op. Her friend Marge would look after him and, that way, he wouldn't get upset seeing the others go. Joyce, Vee and Wib had each given him a big kiss, but they avoided saying goodbye. Siddy had been a little bewildered by all the fuss.

Wib's attentions were concentrated on a blind man with a white stick. There was something odd about him which Wib couldn't quite put his finger on. Maybe it was the strangeness of a man with a white stick blindly trying to pick his way through the mad, bustling crowds. Or maybe it was the way he walked—with a peculiar stoop that made him lean forward almost to the point of toppling over.

The man tapped his way to the barrier and argued with the ticket collector, who, out of sympathy, reluctantly let him through.

Mrs Harris was trying to catch the attention of a tiny W.V.S. lady. The little woman wore a green uniform that looked as if it belonged to someone three times her size. The children knew her; it was Miss Duff.

"Sorry we're late, love," said Mrs Harris. "We got into a terrible two 'n' eight on the trains and had to get a bus in the end because of a land-mine in the tube."

Miss Duff smiled sympathetically. She was the local Sunday School teacher at Gaskill Street Congregational Mission and had bravely, if somewhat foolishly, volunteered to take a group of nearly thirty Hackney children to their new homes. She was carrying the obligatory official clip-board.

"Don't worry, love. Right. Three is it?" She eyed the three Harris children up and down. Vee was wearing her new second-hand coat and beret. She dug at her collar with her finger. She wasn't sure if it was the string of her gas-mask box or the uncomfortably stiff coat material, but she was beginning to get a neck-ache.

Miss Duff checked off her list.

"Gas-mask?"

The children nodded and patted their boxes.

"Label?"

Again they all nodded. Each one of them had a brown parcel label with their name on it, tied on to their lapel. Wib crooked his neck to read the writing on his. It was correct; William Harris, it said, and he reassured himself that that was who he was. Mind you, he only answered to the name Wib so it wouldn't be much use to anybody.

"I don't know why they bother to send us by train. They could have posted us!" Miss Duff, anxious to complete her check list, ignored his joke.

"Spare clothes?"

"Spare clothes," echoed the three of them, tapping their tiny bundles.

"Food for the journey?"

Vee felt the hard lump of the bar of chocolate in her pillow-case. It was a luxury she'd never had before and she dreaded having to finally eat it; somehow it was nicer just knowing it was there. Wib put his head into his pillow-case like a horse nudging its way into a nosebag. His muffled voice answered the question.

"Plenty of food in here." He'd already had a secret nibble of his chocolate on the way to the station. The jam sandwiches he was keeping till later.

"Sensible coat," said Miss Duff, looking at Vee who still didn't like her new coat no matter how 'sensible' it was.

"O.K., then," said Miss Duff, "everything seems to be in order. You're the last so I'll take you down."

"Can I say cheerio now," said Mrs Harris, "or shall I wait till they're on the train?"

"Better do it now I think, love, best get it over and done with."

Mrs Harris grabbed Wib and Vee with both hands and held them close to her.

"Bye, love, be good kids for Mum."

"Bye, Mum."

"Remember to fill in your postcard and let me know just where you're staying. I won't be able to come and see you straight off but Miss Duff here will see you get settled in O.K."

"What about Freddy?" said Vee.

"Well, he'll be coming to the country the moment his ears are better. Now don't go eating your chocolate all at once."

She let go of Vee and Wib and hugged Joyce.

"Joycie, you make sure you look after them."

It was silly pretending not to cry and Joyce, for once, forgot she was the eldest and sobbed on her mother's shoulder. Wib and Vee were a little surprised at this. Joyce had always been the strongest of all of them and it was strange to see her upset. They looked at one another somewhat puzzled, maybe she knew something they didn't. Whatever it was, the sound of Joyce sobbing made the tears well up in Vee and Wib's eyes.

Mrs Harris stroked Joyce's hair.

"Sssh, love. Now don't be silly. You're a big girl now. Don't go upsetting yourself. It won't be for long. They reckon the war will soon be over and then you'll be home again in no time."

Joyce lifted her head up from her mother's shoulder.

"But we haven't got any home, Mum."

"Course we have . . . we *will* have . . . we'll have a nice place by the time you come back. Honest we will. I promise you."

At that moment Miss Duff returned and put her hand on Vee's shoulder.

"We'll have to say cheerio now, Mrs Harris. Three minutes and the train has to go."

Mrs Harris clutched all three children close to her once more. The loudspeaker announced the departure of some obscure train to an even stranger destination, but none of them heard it. Miss Duff repeated her instruction.

"We'll have to go now, Mrs Harris."

The three children pulled away from their mother and moved through the ticket barrier on to Platform 7. Vee and Wib shouted, "Bye," but Joyce kept on running. Mrs Harris pretended not to see them go and fiddled with her coat. Her buttons were already done up, but she did them up once more. Along the platform, steam hissed out from the underbelly of the maroon railway carriage and gobbled up Vee, Wib, Joyce and the diminutive Miss Duff. Mrs Harris looked up from her buttons but could see nothing but railway officials and smoke. She began to walk away, forcing herself not to look back, but when she reached the boarded-up Smith's tobacconists, she could resist no longer. But she saw nothing. The train was beginning to move and the steam obliterated everything.

Joyce leant her head against the window and watched as they left the platform behind. She had not said goodbye because it would have been too final. The tears had made great white streaks on her cheeks and she closed her eyes to stop the station from vanishing into the distance. The lady next to her saw that she was upset. Getting out a knitting bag, she offered Joyce a ball of wool.

"Hold that a jiff, while I wind it up, will you, lovey?"

Wib and Vee weren't quite so lucky as Joyce. Miss Duff hadn't managed to get them a seat, so they had been stuck in the corridor with a crowd of other evacuees who sat on brown cardboard cases, sucked sherbet sticks, and sang long, boring verses of "Ten Green Bottles". Wib snuggled up against a large canvas bag, belonging to an overweight lady wearing a big brown coat with a fox fur collar. The fur had a real fox's head dangling from it, and Wib wondered if it was still alive—its eyes seemed real enough.

Out of the windows of the train Joyce watched the rows and rows of London streets.

They all looked remarkably similar to their own.

Wib spotted a sign which said, "Huntley & Palmer Biscuit Factory" in big letters; he licked his lips as it reminded him of the contents of his pillow-case. He gave a tiny piece of his chocolate to Vee, who was quite astonished at this very rare act of generosity from her brother.

Vee winced as a rather horrible little girl with tight blond curls and a pink ribbon started an impersonation of Shirley Temple, with an absolutely awful rendition of "On The Good Ship Lollypop". Her mother looked on proudly, mouthing each word her daughter sang. She looked around her, basking in any polite compliments that just might come her daughter's way.

Miss Duff negotiated the people in the corridor, trying hard to keep her balance and not succeeding very well. Her bony elbow stuck into the stomach of a soldier who had stood up to let her by. He smiled politely as she knelt down to talk to Vee.

"You all right, love? Nice and comfy?"

"Yes, thanks, Miss Duff."

"Good."

"Excuse me, Miss Duff," asked Vee, "where are we being evacuated to?"

"Not sure, exactly. Somewhere near Bath, I think."

Wib didn't exactly like the sound of "Bath". He imagined a whole town filled with tin baths and wash basins. The thought made him shudder. Miss Duff popped her head in to see that Joyce was settled and then vanished back down the corridor. The soldier breathed in deeply but still Miss Duff managed to poke him in the stomach. Once more he smiled politely—but not as politely as before.

Wib hoisted himself up by the window-strap on the door. It amused him for a while as he pulled the strap off its brass peg, lifting the window up and down. A gush of cold wind rushed through the corridor, annoying the lady with the fox fur and blowing the cap off her little boy.

"Leave off, dear, don't fiddle. Who are you with? Haven't you got your mother looking after you?"

"No, lady, it's not allowed."

"Not allowed?" said the lady, somewhat puzzled. Vee was also a little bewildered; she never quite knew what her brother would be saying next.

"She's in hospital with disease. They wouldn't let her come on trains. Too dangerous."

"Disease?" said the lady, edging away from him slightly and shielding her mouth with her handkerchief.

"Yeah, foxnit's disease. She caught it off a fox fur she used to wear round her neck . . . a bit like yours."

The lady pulled away from him, horrified, not sure if he was joking or not. Vee hid a smile behind her hand.

"It's O.K. It's not catching, lady."

"You lippy little sod. Too much bunny, you've got. If I was your mother I'd put you over my knee."

Wib ignored her and poked his head into the compartment where Joyce was sitting.

"Joycie, can I go for a walk?"

"No, stay where you are."

"But I'm fed up."

"Count the telegraph poles. We'll be in the country in a minute. You can look out of the window."

Wib breathed on to the glass partition and drew a face with his finger. It was then he heard the tap tap of a stick. He spun round to see the blind man from the station stepping over Vee. Wib was intrigued and watched him walk up the corridor. There was something about his blindness that disturbed him. It was the way he stepped over the people sitting on the floor. Not once did he accidentally tread on someone's foot or bump into the side.

"That blind man's a bit fishy, Vee. I'm sure of it."

Vee yawned and took out her *Beano* to read. She didn't even look up.

"Don't tell me—he's a German."

"Don't laugh. He could be."

"Belt up and read your *Dandy*," said Vee, "I'll swop you when I've read this."

Wib didn't read his *Dandy* but he did look out of the train window and count the telegraph poles. After a while he got quite dizzy trying to follow the wires from pole to pole. The curly-haired little girl was now doing a full tap dance routine on top of her mother's case. The other kids, soldiers and nurses had long since become bored by the performance. Her mother on the other hand still faithfully mouthed encouragement as her daughter sang.

"Sparkle, Shirley, sparkle," she exclaimed at regular intervals.

Suddenly the little girl stopped dancing and squeezed her knees together—her mother was aghast.

"What's the matter, Shirley? Why have you stopped?" Poor little Shirley started to cry.

"Lav, Mum. I want to go to the lav."

"Course you don't. You haven't finished your song yet."

"Mum, I've got to go right away."

"Why?"

"'Cause I've already started . . .!"

There was a slight commotion at Shirley's revelation. A soldier quickly picked her up and handed her over the heads of the other children to a W.V.S. lady, who led her to the room marked "Toilet" at the end of the corridor. Wib nearly split himself laughing at blond Shirley's predicament.

He decided to explore a little and discovered an ingenious method of getting down the corridor. He noticed that if he crawled on his hands and knees there was almost a tunnel through the piles of cases, packages and bags. By wriggling extra carefully through the tiniest gaps, he managed to reach the end.

He stood up to get his bearings, then he walked through an enormous rubber concertina that joined the two carriages. On the floor he spotted a box of Swan Vestas matches. Instinctively he picked the box up and shook it. To his surprise it rattled—there were still matches inside. He looked around him to see if anyone was watching, then quickly popped it into his picture card tin.

Through the train windows Wib could see that the crowded grey streets were beginning to give way to green fields—the greenest he had ever seen. For a while he wasn't bored any more as he stared in total wonderment at the huge open spaces. He soon realised he wasn't alone. Vee had joined him and he looked at her out of the corner of his eye.

"There's no people, Vee! Or houses. Just grass, loads and loads of grass. Bigger than Victoria Park, even!"

"That's what the country is, clever—grass. Well, mostly."

"But there's no swing gardens or back alleys to play in. Look! There's a pig," shouted Wib.

"It's a sheep," insisted Vee.

"It's a pig. Look there's hundreds of 'em."

"They're sheep. You don't get that many pigs." Vee was adamant. "Anyway pigs are pink not white. Sheep are white."

An elderly lady was listening to their conversation with great amusement.

"They're cows, love."

"Cows?" Vee and Wib were stunned into silence. They were extremely embarrassed about knowing so little of the world they were soon to be living in.

At that moment the train went into a tunnel and they were plunged into total darkness.

"I didn't know these trains went underground."

The two of them looked at the black wall of the tunnel as it rushed by. Out in the light once more, stations whizzed past at regular intervals, but it was impossible to read their names.

The flat green fields soon became steep hillsides with animals (Vee and Wib dare not risk naming them) dotted across them. To Wib the houses seemed to be perched, almost balancing, up in the air.

"You'd think the houses would roll down the hill," said Wib.

Vee didn't answer him. She'd stopped

looking out of the window and had turned her attention to the corridor.

"Wib, look at that man."

Wib followed her glance and saw the blind man with the stoop who he'd noticed earlier.

"Already seen him. Saw him ages ago."

"Look at him now."

"I told you he was fishy when I saw him at the station."

"Can you see though, what I can see?"

Wib stared at the man who was sitting in the corner, away from everybody else. His white stick was lying between his knees. Wib just shrugged.

"No. He just looks fishy. Don't know why."

"But he's reading! He's reading the paper."

Wib swung his head round like the boy in the Persil advertisements. Sure enough, the man had lifted up his steel-framed, dark glasses and was busily reading the *News Chronicle*. As he turned the pages, he seemed to sense them looking at him. Vee and Wib swung back and pretended to look out of the window, but their curiosity had moved away from the cows and sheep and had firmly fixed on Old Stoopy with the white stick. The blind man who wasn't.

CHAPTER 9
FLICKS AT THE PALACE

The train had slowed down almost to a halt when Joyce yanked them back to their places. The railway sign outside the door said "Whistle", so Wib whistled a few bars of "Umbrella Man".

The train chugged into action once more and eased its way slowly into a station.

"Where are we?" Wib was the first with the question but everybody was surprised that they'd stopped. Vee poked her head out of the window and tried to read the station sign. It had been white-washed over at the beginning of the war to confuse the Germans, but so far it had only managed to confuse the English. A layer of dust had formed on the tops of the letters and Vee was just able to make out the word.

"Does it say Bath?" asked Wib.

"No. It's a longer word . . . Patney . . . and . . . Churton."

"Patney and Churton? Never heard of it."

Out on the platform W.V.S. ladies and railway officials were deep in conversation. There were childrens' heads poking out of every window, awaiting the outcome. Miss Duff came into their carriage and announced the news.

"Right, Harris family—off you get and form

up on the platform, please."

"Is this where we've been evacuated to, Miss Duff?" asked Vee.

"No. We're getting another train—half of us are taking the branch line to Devizes, the rest are going on to Bath. Wib had never heard of Devizes but at least it didn't sound quite as suspect as Bath.

The children queued up in long straggly lines along the platform and waved goodbye to their companions. As the train vanished around the bend, they sat down on their cases. Already the branch line train could be seen in the distance, chugging towards them. It was then that Wib noticed Old Stoopy. He hadn't got off the train the platform side, instead he had jumped onto the open line and could be seen scrambling up the grassy verge, chased by two railway officials.

"Look, Vee. Old Stoopy! Joycie, look, it's the blind man," Wib said, as the man struggled up the bank with his cases. His coat flapped open to reveal a uniform underneath.

"He's a deserter!"

"Who are you talking about?" said Joyce, a little annoyed at being dug in the ribs by her brother.

Vee answered her but Joyce didn't hear. The train thundered into the station and Old Stoopy disappeared in the distance, leaving the railway officials far behind on the embankment.

The branch line journey was not quite so

crowded and Vee and Wib both had seats of their own. It was a good opportunity to stretch their feet out and do justice to the jam sandwiches, which the three of them consumed in record time.

It was beginning to get dark when they got to Devizes. There were half-a-dozen policemen waiting on the station with big welcoming smiles but, as yet, no sign of a welcoming cup of tea. Again Miss Duff organised them into neat rows. The Devizes sign had also been painted white, but apart from this there was little indication of the war in the small country station. Bright advertisement posters were neatly stuck everywhere. "California Syrup for the Bowels", said one. "If your breath has a smell, you can't feel well", said another, which made Wib smile. On the other hand he didn't like the sound of "Clarke's Blood Mixture — amputation avoided".

About fifty children and half-a-dozen mothers filed out of the white gate and, in a long ragged procession, made their way up the hill to the centre of town.

In the half-light the children could see the old country buildings quite clearly.

"Looks like an old prison," said Wib to Vee as they passed a large building with the words "Corn Exchange" written across it in big, faded gold letters. At the top of the hill was the Devizes Market Square, in the centre of which was an attractive ornamental fountain and, close by, a rather ugly-looking ancient monument. The procession crossed the road by The Pelican pub and weaved its way past Strong's Tea Room and yet another pub, called The Black Swan.

"It's all bloody pubs," said Wib.

"We'll be all right for pies," answered Vee, as they passed a pie shop. Vee's words were a little optimistic because the strange pie-making machine lay idle, covered in dust in the window. There was a sign saying: "Sorry no pies." Another said, "Snow White and the Seven Dwarves: Meritous Production at Mission Hall in aid of Lord Mayor of London's Distress Fund for Evacuees." The last words were a little cheering.

"That means *us*," said Vee, pleased that Londoners would be welcome in this strange country town.

"At least they seem to like us," said Joyce.

"Like who?"

"Londoners. I mean you hear some funny stories in places."

"What kind of stories?" asked Wib.

"Like country people not liking people from London," said Vee.

"Well, they'll have to like us and lump us—else we'll be on the first train home—suits me."

Suddenly the procession came to a halt as the policeman at the front waved then into the Palace cinema. Wib couldn't believe their luck.

"We're going to the flicks."

The long, tired faces of all the children began to perk up a little at the thought of going to the pictures. A poster in the foyer advertised the current programme: "*All At Sea* with Sandy Powell and Kay Walsh. Supporting feature: *Gene Autry, the singing cowboy.*"

Inside, the small cinema had been converted into a temporary rest centre. There were trestle tables in the aisles and posh ladies in neat dresses standing behind steaming saucepans, full of soup. The children piled into the darkened interior and found themselves a comfortable seat.

At the front a tall, skinny gentleman in a crumpled grey suit was helped up on to the stage by two policemen. He held a metal petrol funnel that he was proposing to use as a megaphone. He coughed loudly to get attention but everyone was busy chatting, sorting out their gas-mask cases and checking their precious bits and pieces. Miss Duff stood up to quieten the noisy children.

"Sssh! Be quiet! The gentleman wants to say something."

The man with the make-shift megaphone started to speak, rather nervously.

"Er . . . my name is N. Fishpool."

There was a ripple of laughter at this but Mr Fishpool continued unaffected.

"In my capacity as Town Clerk of Devizes, I would like to welcome you all on behalf of the council, the W.V.S., and Mr Gozzard's Reception Committee, to out beautiful town. I know you've had an exhausting journey, leaving behind . . . er . . . loved ones, etcetera, and so Mrs Edkins and her good ladies here would be delighted if you would tuck into some soup, some bread and . . . *butter.*'' There was a ripple of enthusiasm from the evacuees at this last revelation.

''It makes a change from marge, I dare say.'' Mr Fishpool laughed at his own joke and a few of the children joined in.

''Right then, I'll not detain you any longer. I'm sure you're all famished.''

''Where we going to stay, mister?'' yelled someone.

A rough-looking woman rasped out from the back of the cinema.

''Where's our houses?''

Mr Fishpool was the kind of man who, although he ruffled easily, would never be impolite.

''Er . . . we will be issuing blankets afterwards and Mr Austin, the manager of this cinema, has kindly loaned us the Palace for the night. Our billeting officer, Mrs Knapp-Jenkins, will be ferrying you out to your new billets in the morning.''

There was an excited babble of noise from the children when they heard the news.

''Can we see a film, mister?'' said a small boy with a loud voice. Mr Fishpool threw a nervous glance towards Mr Austin, who waved his arms indicating an emphatic No.

"Er . . . I'm afraid not, children . . ."

Before he could finish, the fifty Londoners erupted.

"Why not?"

"You rotten lot!"

"Put the flick on, don't be a spoil-sport."

The noise was quite frightening and Mr Fishpool whispered loudly to Mr Austin.

"You'll have to let them see something, Dennis!"

Mr Austin reluctantly agreed and made off in the direction of his projection box. He muttered to himself, obviously a little irritated. Evacuees or not, one free showing meant fifty less tickets he would be selling next week.

Wib, Joyce and Vee slept very well that night. The train journey had tired them out but the hot soup and free film had revived them somewhat and rounded off their evening nicely. It was a bit difficult getting comfortable at first, but Vee and Joyce snuggled up close and were soon asleep. Wib stretched himself out across one aisle and people, on the way to the toilets, stepped over him all night long.

The next morning Miss Duff helped the billeting officer, Mrs Knapp-Jenkins, sort out the children. One by one, they went off down the aisle and out of the door marked "EXIT".

Miss Duff called out for Wib to come forward.

"William Harris, please."

"No. I have to be with me sisters." Wib was dumbstruck. It never occurred to him that they might split up. Joyce spoke up.

"We have to stay together, miss, me Mum made me promise."

Miss Duff checked her list once more and went into a huddle with the billeting officer.

"All right, you can go together," said Mrs Knapp-Jenkins. "But you might have to make arrangements when you get there."

The three of them stepped out of the dark cinema into the bright daylight of the market square. Outside was a brewer's cart, pulled by two giant grey and white shire horses. On the side of the cart were the words "Wadsworth Brewery—Finest Ales".

There were already a dozen or so children sitting on top. The three Harris children were helped up by an enormous man with white hair and ruddy cheeks. His hand and arm felt like iron as he lifted them.

"That's the lot, Mr Jobart," said the billeting lady, as he helped her on to the front seat.

"Giddy-yup, Mavis, giddy-yup, Martha!"

Martha and Mavis obliged and the brewery cart lurched away from the kerb.

A few miles outside Devizes the cart stopped at a five-bar gate. On it was tied a sign: "Torney End Farm. Trespassers will be prosecuted." Not much of a welcome, thought Wib.

"John and Irene Kennedy?" said Mrs Knapp-Jenkins. Two children at the back of the cart timidly raised their hands.

"Off you come, dear. Torney End is where you're billeted."

The two children picked up their bags and vanished down the lane with Mrs Knapp-Jenkins.

"What does 'billeted' mean, Joycie?" asked Wib.

"Something to do with the place you're going to stay," guessed Joyce.

"Why don't they talk plain English in war-time?" grumbled Wib.

The brewer's cart continued on its way and the sun shone warmly on their faces as, one by one, the children were dropped off at different farms.

In his position high on the cart Wib could see over the tops of the hedges. He spotted sheep and cows in every field. As he had suspected, there were no back alleys, but he had to admit there seemed to be so many other interesting playgrounds, hide-aways, gulleys, copses, broken-down barns, all offering up no end of possibilities for boyish mischief. It was then he saw the biggest surprise yet. The brewer's cart had gone over a small hump-backed bridge, revealing a network of locks and canals.

"Canals! Look, Vee, Joycie. Locks like at Hackney! Only more of them. Dozens of 'em. Look."

"Oh, ah, that's the Kennet and Avon Canal, son," said Mr Jobart, in his croaky Wiltshire accent. Wib was so overjoyed he nearly toppled off the cart, as it turned sharply into a narrow road.

"Look at that, Joycie. What is it?"

Vee pointed to a strange stone monument that marked the corner. On top of it was a man with one arm, who seemed to peer down on them as they passed. Once more their guide, Mr Jobart, croaked the answer.

"He was quite an important man in this village a couple of hundred years ago, name of Sir Percival Squill. He said he'd give his right arm for a good road to the village. You see in those days everyone had to travel miles over that big hill to get to it—anyway, the council built this road about fifty years ago and suddenly one night the statue's right arm fell off. Hooligans the police said, but the locals say old Squill was haunting it."

Mrs Knapp-Jenkins noticed the slightly worried look on the Londoners' faces and laughed out loud.

"Don't you go listening to Mr Jobart, he's full of stories—old brewer's tales. Here we are. Pottley."

The cart pulled to a halt in front of an old stone horse-trough and Martha and Mavis plunged their heads in the water.

Pottley was a very pretty village with one straightish road you could vaguely call a high street, which had tiny old-fashioned shops dotted all along it. Above them, on top of a slight hill, was the church and in front of them, a small school.

A round-faced man emerged from the post office on the corner. He had a big beer-drinker's stomach, held in with a thick leather belt, and bandy legs that seemed to have, understandably, buckled under the weight of his bulky body. He stepped up to the horse cart and respectfully took off his hat to Mrs Knapp-Jenkins.

"Hello, Mrs Napkins."

Mrs Knapp-Jenkins frowned at his mispronounciation of her name, and was quick to correct him.

"Knapp-Jenkins."

"Oh, ah. You got here all right, then."

"Morning, Bixey. These are your new lodgers."

"Three, ma'am?" said old Bixey. "I think Miss Doughbridge is only expecting two."

"We were told two and two, but the fourth child is in hospital so perhaps you could squeeze the three of them in. It seems silly to split them up."

Too true, thought Wib. It was more than

''silly'' to him, it was an impossibility. He was sticking to Vee and Joyce, no matter what.

''It's O.K. with Mrs Bixey and me of course, but I'll have to ask Miss Doughbridge first, ma'am.''

He leaned forward to shake Joyce's hand. His own hands were knobbly and hard, like old leather left in the sun. They were farmer's hands, used to hard work.

''Welcome to Pottley,'' he said.

''Thank you,'' Joyce replied, quickly pulling her hand out of the knobbly vice.

''I'm Joyce Harris. This here is Veronica and William.''

Vee and Wib looked at one another in amazement. No one ever called them by their real names—certainly not Joyce. They nodded to Mr Bixey.

''Bye-bye,'' said Mrs Knapp-Jenkins.

''Watch out for old Squill,'' shouted Mr Jobart, ''his horse drinks at this trough so they say. Ha! ha!''

He went even redder in the face as he laughed, and had to tug at the reins to keep his balance.

Mr Bixey picked up the children's bundles and led them off down the lane between the school and the post office.

''Small school, Joycie,'' said Wib.

''It's a small place,'' answered Vee quickly, if a little obviously.

"You like the country, you kids?" said Mr Bixey, trying to put them at ease.

"We don't know yet, we've never been before," replied Wib abruptly.

"Where is this place exactly, Mr Bixey?" Vee was determined to be polite.

"Pottley and Little Echilton, the village is called, and you're going to stay at our farm, or rather Miss Doughbridge's farm."

Wib didn't like the sound of Miss Doughbridge already. It sounded like a school teacher's name—"Old Drawbridge".

"Are we far from London?" asked Vee.

Mr Bixey laughed.

"Oh, I should say so, my dear. This here is Wiltshire—good hundred miles from London, we are. Thank the Lord."

Wib whistled. A hundred miles, he thought. It sounded like the other side of the world. Just then Mr Bixey stopped at a big puddle that had spread across the full width of the lane. It was quite the biggest puddle they'd ever seen. Mr Bixey carried on walking through it, in his Wellington boots. The three Harris children just stood there looking at the puddle. There was no way they could walk through it in their plimsolls.

"All right, stay where you are, young 'uns." Mr Bixey ploughed back through the water and, one at a time, helped them across into the dry. Ten yards further on he stopped once more.

"Right. Here we are, young 'uns—home."

The three children looked through the gateway towards a large, grand old house that was covered in pretty yellow flowers. To one side of the entrance-way was another gate that led to a small, white-fronted, thatched farmhouse. It all looked very strange to them. They'd never seen open spaces, sheep, cows or pigs in their lives before. It wasn't near anything, anywhere or anyone they'd ever known. It was over a hundred miles apart from Mum, and a whole world apart from No. 8 Paxton Street. Yet this man Bixey was calling it their "home". It gave them an odd feeling.

CHAPTER 10
BUTT'S FARM AND OVEN BOTTOM

Mr Bixey beckoned them to follow him into the driveway of the grand-looking house. A very neat sign was nailed to the front wall, and Vee nudged Joyce to read it. It said, "This Way BUTT'S HOUSE. That Way (with an appropriate arrow) BUTT'S FARM. Absolutely no admittance to unauthorised persons. Proprietor: Miss M. Doughbridge." Whoever "Old Drawbridge" was, thought Wib, she wasn't short of a bob or two, and she obviously didn't like visitors.

Mr Bixey knocked on the door of Butt's House. Joyce noticed that he nervously rubbed his wellington boots on the backs of his brown corduroy trousers and dragged his fingers through his wispy, blond hair, in a vain effort to smarten himself up. He needn't have bothered; his pudgy, irregular features gave his face a permanently untidy look. But there was a kindness in his smile that put them at ease. The three Harris children looked all around them as they waited for the door to be answered. Everywhere had been kept absolutely immaculately. There were neat lawns and neat flower beds and neat walls with pretty plants climbing all over them in well-trained lines.

Mr Bixey knocked on the door once again. This time it opened slowly, but not much. He edged up closer to the door and whispered to someone inside. Joyce screwed up her eyes to get a better look but all she could see was a shadowy figure.

"Er . . . excuse me, Miss Liggerty, but could you tell Miss Doughbridge that the evacuees are here and that there's more than the two we expected. There's one extra, a little lad . . . Mrs Bixey's only made up two beds, you see."

"You'll have to make do for tonight. We'll talk about it later. Miss Doughbridge is taking her nap at the moment."

"Yes, ma'am." Mr Bixey respectfully put his cap back on his head and the shadowy figure of Miss Liggerty vanished into the darkness. She closed the door with a soft but precise click.

"What a funny lady," Vee whispered to Joyce, who was thinking the same thing. Mr Bixey hoisted up his corduroy trousers and tucked them under his thick leather belt.

"Right. Let's get you across to meet my Fay—Mrs Bixey, that is. This way."

The three children followed him out of the gate and into the farmyard, which in contrast to Butt's House was muddy and very messy. Wib looked back to the house and noticed a strange figure at the upstairs window. It had a pale, colourless face with grey hair. Was it Miss Doughbridge? Whoever it was, he or she quickly pulled the lace curtain across when they saw Wib looking.

Chickens clucked and fluttered out of the way as Joyce and Vee squelched across the muddy yard. Vee walked over to examine the birds a little more closely. She'd seen pictures of chickens but never before had she seen one at close quarters—except at Christmas, that is. But this one was different; it was alive and kicking and it strutted in front of Vee, twisting its head sharply in different directions, although never once taking its eyes off her.

Wib wasn't looking where he was going and trod in something nasty, left behind by one of the cows. He examined the green slime on his plimsoll.

"I've really put me foot in it this time, Joycie!"

Joyce and Vee turned their noses up. Opening the door of the white-fronted farmhouse, Mr Bixey held his arm out to welcome them in. At that moment a big black dog leapt out and started licking him.

"Now get down, Jip. There's a good boy. I know you're pleased to see me but we've got visitors. Fay! Are you there, Fay? Our little lodgers have arrived."

Mr Bixey turned towards the children.

"Well, come on in then. Don't be shy. Jip won't bite you."

"We're not scared of dogs, mister," said Wib. "We've got a dog just like him at home in London. Well, used to have—only he went missing.''

"That's good, then. I've no doubt you and Jip will be really good mates by the time you have to be going home."

The four of them stepped into the tiny hall. Joyce smiled at Vee, not for any real reason but because she sensed immediately that it was a nice house. It was warm and cosy, with a big roaring fire in the lounge and the wonderful smell of homemade bread wafting out from the kitchen.

Mr Bixey called out for his wife once more.

"Fay! Where the devil is that woman? Fay, our visitors have arrived. Oh, there you are."

At the top of the narrow stairs appeared a short, very short (no bigger than Vee), stout lady who was almost as wide as she was tall. Her fat, rosy country cheeks glowed, even as far away as the top of the stairs. She dropped the linen she was carrying and trotted down to meet them.

"Well, very pleased to meet you, I'm sure. I've been getting the beds ready . . . I hope you like your room. It's not very big but it's nice and cosy. I've had the fire going up there for an hour, so the beds should be nice and aired."

She gabbled on a bit because she was probably more nervous at the sight of the children than they were of her. She also seemed to have trouble catching her breath, as tubby people often do. Suddenly she noticed Wib, who had been hidden by the grandfather clock.

"Wilf, there's three of them. I thought Mrs

Knapp-hyphen-Whatsit said only two for the time being.''

Joyce spoke up. ''He's our brother, you see, missus, and they originally were going to put him in with our other brother but he got caught by a bomb blast—Freddy that is, our other brother—and it didn't do his ears any good so they took him away to the hospital and we came away without him—so Wib's by himself and we don't want him left on his own.''

Joyce drew a deep breath after getting through her long explanation. Wib smiled at the lady in an effort to win her round. He wasn't sure that he trusted her yet, but he didn't fancy being split from Vee and Joyce, either.

Their bedroom was very small but there was a fireplace against one wall and the banked-up fire threw out a glow that made the room look and feel very inviting.

There was one metal bedstead against the wall and an old sideboard with a china jug and bowl on top. The walls were covered in a neat patterned wallpaper and there was a coloured picture of a little girl stroking a St. Bernard dog, with three angels looking over her shoulder.

''You'd better unpack your things,'' said Mrs Bixey, ''and hang them up in the cupboard.''

''We haven't brought much, Mrs Bixey,'' said Joyce. ''We were bombed out, see, and we lost all our clothes.''

''What we're wearing's not even ours,'' Vee

quickly added. "They gave us this stuff at the reception centre."

"Oh well, we'll probably be able to fix you up with a few things," said Mrs Bixey.

She pulled a case from under the bed and took out a lot of very old-fashioned clothes.

"That'll do us fine," said Joyce, but as usual Vee turned her nose up behind Mrs Bixey's back.

"I'll have to make the young lad up a bed on the floor. I hope you won't mind, love."

"Oh, he won't mind, Mrs Bixey," Joyce answered, before Wib could offer an opinion.

"And now," said Mrs Bixey, "I expect you'll want your dinner. Toad-in-the-hole all right for you?"

It sounded delicious, and it was. Mrs Bixey's homemade sausages were the meatiest thing they'd ever tasted; as for the batter pudding, well it really did melt in the mouth, like it says in the advertisements.

Wib patted his full stomach and looked across to Mr Bixey. He wondered if his paunch would get as big as the farmer's by the end of their stay. He'd certainly eaten far too much homemade bread.

Mrs Bixey took out yet another dish from the oven of her black kitchen range.

"Fruit pie? Now I know you'll be able to squeeze a little slice down you."

Joyce smiled. "I thought there was supposed

to be food rationing, Mrs Bixey."

"Ah, well, that's where us country people does best, you see—grows most of it ourselves. Short of one or two things, mind—there's a lot we can't get now."

Joyce looked down at the enormous fruit pie and, next to it, a basin full of hot custard. Mrs Bixey gave Vee a wooden spoon.

"Stir that for me, love, don't let it get lumpy."

Mr Bixey eased himself back in his chair and lit up his pipe.

"No pie for me, Fay, I'm just about full."

"You can say that again," said Wib.

"My Fay is the best cook in Pottley, so you've struck lucky here, young 'uns. Oh, ah."

The three of them smiled at the thought. Wib had lots of questions to ask Mr Bixey about Pottley but was stopped in his tracks by a bell that started ringing over the fireplace. Mr Bixey got up quickly and walked to the black stove to tap out his pipe. Joyce's eyes followed the string that worked the bell. It trailed across the ceiling, out of the door and then across the yard.

"Miss Doughbridge will be wanting me," said Bixey, putting on his jacket. "Won't be a couple of ticks. Now you lot tuck in. I don't want to see anything left on those plates when I come back, do you hear me? Oh, ah."

He went out of the door, combing his hair with his fingers as he went.

"Who is this Miss Doughbridge then, Mrs Bixey?" asked Vee.

"She's our landlady. She owns this farm. And a couple of others."

"And all the animals, too?"

"All the animals, all the land, all the tractors, everything. And us," she chuckled. "She's a very rich lady is our Miss Doughbridge."

"Who's Miss Lig . . . Liggy?" Joyce asked.

"Liggerty. She's Miss Doughbridge's companion—she sort of looks after her. She had an accident, you see—got run down by a tractor in the high street. Terrible to-do there was. Court case and all. She never got her leg back."

Vee and Wib burst out laughing at this remark. Joyce was embarrassed.

"Ssh! Don't be rude, you two."

But Mrs Bixey had also seen the funny side.

"Never got her leg back to normal, I mean. She has to use a stick. Plays her up something rotten, her leg does, and when that happens, well . . ."

Mrs Bixey waved her hand and pulled a face to denote the ceiling falling in.

"Can we help you wash up, Mrs Bixey?" said Joyce.

"No, love. I suggest you do a little exploring. Find your way around. Why don't you take a walk up to the village? You can cut across the fields by Oven Bottom."

Wib nearly knocked his chair over in his eagerness to get out of the door. Vee and Joyce followed him. They had no idea where or what Oven Bottom was, but it sounded too good to miss.

"Bye, Mrs Bixey. See you later."

"Don't be too late, mind."

"No. We promise."

The three children ran out into the farmyard and disappeared into the first barn. It had a dark interior that smelt of cows, and many other things which Wib, once more, accidentally put his foot in. There were concrete pens, with a strange contraption made of water pipes and wooden ladders that led up to dark, secret lofts. Wib ran straight up the nearest ladder and came down even faster by jumping on to a pile of hay to break his fall.

Joyce opened up another door, revealing a long chicken coop. The chickens squawked at the intruder and gave her a rather superior look as they went about their business.

"Look, Joycie!" said Vee, pointing at the cluster that one of the hens had left behind. "Real eggs!"

The old gate at the bottom of the yard presented no problems for Wib, who leapt over it. Joyce and Vee climbed over a little more elegantly. The field was the biggest open space they had ever been in, and they ran down the slight slope as fast as their plimsolled feet would carry them. Joyce shouted out every sort of silly thought that came into her head, until she was hoarse. Wib sang ''Umbrella Man'' as loud as he had ever dared—with not a soul to tell him to shut up. Vee was as brave as she'd ever been, inviting the great woolly sheep to shake her hand. Naturally, most of them declined.

Oven Bottom was a small hillock at the bottom of the field, and over the stone wall was a narrow but very deep gully that cut through the fields, winding its way almost up to the back door of the post office. The gully was quickly re-named ''Cheddar Gorge'' by Vee; this would be their short cut to school.

The stone-walled paddock behind the post office was the home of an elderly horse that Wib christened ''Champion'', after Gene Autrey's best friend. If ever there was a horse less like a film star's, it was this sad individual.

They ran down the cobbled alley, in between the Pottley post office and the undertaker's yard, and found themselves in the high street. A man riding a bicycle waved to them as they emerged from the alleyway.

''Evening.''

''Evening,'' said the three Londoners, as if they'd known him for ages. Up past the war memorial and the stone horse-trough, and there it was, opposite St. Mary's Church: their new school.

''It's ever so small, Joycie. Can't hold more than twenty kids,'' said Wib.

"Pretty, though. Quite nice." Vee was beginning to like it at Pottley.

"No school can be nice," countered Wib.

They walked quickly down the rest of the street, examining the shops: Spicer's the barbers; Bootwick's Smithy (which had been crossed out and re-named Bootwick's Motor Repairs); Belcher's hardware store; Noblock's the grocer; Madame Sonia the ladies hairdressers; The Bell Inn; The George & Dragon; The Salvation Army Mission Hall; there was even Perrymead 'the animal feed purveyor', whatever that was.

"Race you back to the horse-trough," said Joyce, getting a good five yard start on the other two. Chiselled into the side of the trough was an inscription: "Donated by public subscription for parched horses in the village of Pottley and Little Echilton." Wib wasn't a horse, or particularly parched, but he still cupped his hand and took a mouthful of the water. Surprisingly, it tasted quite nice.

Down Urchley Lane they ran, past the thatched house, Great Western cottages, Frogshitch Farm and into Butt's Lane. This time they ran along the high bank to avoid the giant puddles.

Back at Butt's Farm the chickens wisely scampered out of the path of the new lodgers. Inside, Mr and Mrs Bixey sat at the table, drinking tea and munching scones. Mr Bixey's ready smile wasn't quite so convincing as they all piled into the small kitchen.

"Hello, young 'uns, get a good look at the village of ours?"

"We went as far as the motor repairers."

"Well, there's not much after that, just Castleton Farm," said Mr Bixey, stirring his tea and puffing a cloud of pipe smoke into the air. He cleared his throat as people often do when they've got something difficult to say.

"I've . . . er . . . had a word with Miss Doughbridge and she thinks it's better the lad sleeps over there." He pointed in the direction of Butt's House.

"What just for tonight?" asked Joyce.

"No. For your stay in Pottley."

"How long will that be?"

"Only Mr Churchill knows that, young 'un!"

"But I want to be with Joycie and Vee."

"Well, it seems Miss Doughbridge doesn't think it's right, cramming the three of you into one room—what with her having so many spare rooms and all. So she's had Miss Liggerty make you up a bed."

Wib stared at the flagstoned floor. He'd only been in the Bixey's house for an hour or so, but he already felt at home. It gave off a warm glow whereas Miss Doughbridge's house felt sinister and cold. On top of that, there was Mrs Bixey's cooking.

"Will I come here for me dinners, missus?"

"I don't know, love," replied Mrs Bixey. "I think Miss Doughbridge will decide that."

"Better get your things, young 'un, and I'll take you over straight 'way."

"We won't be far away, Wib." Joyce tried to console him, but he was beginning to get quite tearful.

"Mum told you to keep us together and now you're splitting us up."

"But it's only across the farmyard!"

This was too much for Wib who dashed off up the narrow wooden stairs to the bedroom. Vee, Joyce and Mrs Bixey stood silently looking at one another, and Mr Bixey nervously jangled the keys in his pocket. Wib returned with his pillow case and his coat over his arm.

"We'll see you in the morning, Wib," said Joyce. But Wib wasn't talking to her. Mrs Bixey by way of consolation offered up a plate of scones.

"Scone, love?"

"I don't want your bloody scones. You can stick 'em!" Wib knocked the plate up in the air, out of Mrs Bixey's hands, and the scones went everywhere. Mr Bixey put his strong hand on to Wib's shoulder and guided him to the door.

"Come on, lad, off we go. There's a big lad. No tears now."

Wib and Mr Bixey walked across the yard, past the old iron water pump and up the path to the door of Butt's House. It was only about ten yards, but it seemed like miles to poor Wib.

CHAPTER 11
FROG EYES AND DOREEN NOBLOCK

The first thing Wib noticed about Miss Liggerty was that she wore steel-framed spectacles, magnifying her eyes to twice the size of a normal person's so that they stuck out like two whelks on Isaac's jellied-eel stall.

She spoke with a slow drawl that indicated she had something wrong with her mouth; it hung down slightly on the left, making her face a little lop-sided.

''Come with me, please.''

Wib obeyed, following her up the large, shiny wooden staircase that smelled of Mansion Polish and cats. There were pictures all the way up depicting various religious scenes, and reminding Wib of Sunday school.

At the top of the dark stairs, he could see a frail figure silhouetted against the light of the gas lamp. But he couldn't see a face. In fact, for a second, he thought that she didn't have one, but he put that out of his mind as it frightened him. Out of the shadows came a pale, white hand and a long, bony finger beckoned him to follow down the narrow corridor. Miss Liggerty took one of the old lady's hands and helped her along. On the other side she supported herself with a stick, walking slowly and dragging her right leg. Wib was sure this was Old Drawbridge.

Liggerty lit the gas mantle in his room and the yellow glow illuminated Miss Doughbridge's white face. It was thick with powder and, but for red lipstick signposting a mouth, she hardly had any features at all.

Wib, absolutely terrified, stood in the doorway—almost afraid to step into the same room with these two strange women.

"Got a name, have you?" said Miss Doughbridge, in a haughty upper-class accent.

Wib nodded, but didn't speak.

"Lost your tongue, lad?"

Wib shook his head.

"Come on now, you must have a name."

Wib gulped to get his vocal chords working. "Wib."

"Wib?" queried the lady with the lop-sided face and whelk eyes.

"It's short for William."

"Bill is short for William."

"No, my dad's already Bill—so they called me Wib."

"I don't approve of nick-names," interrupted Miss Doughbridge. "A Christian name is a given name and what's given in the name of Jesus should be kept. Well, William, this is your room. There's water in the jug for you to have a good wash and then I suggest you go to bed. Miss Liggerty will waken you in the morning for breakfast.''

''Can't I have breakfast with me sisters, missus?''

''No. Miss Liggerty will be looking after you from now on. Mrs Bixey has got quite enough on her hands with two children. Now if you'd like to kneel and say your prayers, you can go to bed. Come on, kneel down, lad.''

Wib knelt down and put his hands together. He looked up at Miss Doughbridge and Miss Liggerty who waited for him to begin.

''Er . . . I don't know no prayers, missus. They don't tell prayers in Hackney. I don't know no verses . . .''

Miss Doughbridge put her hands together and closed her eyes.

''Lord keep us safe this night, secure from all our fears. May angels guard us while we sleep till morning light appears. Amen.''

''Amen,'' said Wib weakly. That much he knew.

''Tomorrow Miss Liggerty will write it out for you so that you can learn it off by heart. Good night, William, put out the gas before you go to sleep.''

The door closed and the two women shuffled down the corridor. Wib climbed on to the high brass bed and pulled his pillow-case close to him. He felt his tin of picture cards through the thin material. It was his only comfort as he stared at the hissing gas lamp. He was in no hurry to put it out. Being along in this cold, eerie room in the dark was just about as miserable a thought as he could conjure up. He looked at one of the religious pictures on the wall. It showed a lot of children dressed as angels, and underneath it said, "Suffer little children."

He was suffering all right, he thought. But, much to his disgust, the soft feather mattress was very comfortable and soon he was fast asleep.

As the three children ran through the "Cheddar Gorge" on their way to school the next morning, Vee went through each item she and Joyce had eaten for breakfast.

". . . then we had toast and marmalade, with great chunks of fruit in it."

"Two eggs?" Wib asked Vee once more. His voice was a little disbelieving and tinged with envy.

"That's right," Vee confirmed.

"What *each*?"

"Each—and a pot of tea to ourselves."

Wib didn't take the news very well. He'd had a bowl of lumpy porridge and a cup of tea that was cold by the time he got to drink it. Old "Whelkie" Liggerty was obviously not much of a cook, and as for Old Drawbridge, she never seemed to eat anything.

In the alley at the side of the post office Vee stopped briefly to stroke Champion, but Wib was more interested in the coffin lids in the undertaker's yard.

"Come on, you two," said Joyce. "We don't want to be late on our first morning."

Joyce pushed open the iron gate that led into the school playground. It seemed very similar to Paxton Street School, smaller of course, but otherwise very familiar. There was a square block of outside toilets and a metal water fountain with a steel cup on a chain. Even the games looked the same; a crowd of children were playing "Warney-Echo" up against the railings (except they called it "Donkey"). There was Hop-Scotch, Two Balls, Skipping, British Bulldog, Five-Stones, Sticky Toffee and, much to Wib's delight, a game of picture cards.

The local children eyed the Londoners suspiciously as they walked in. A tubby, round-faced girl came up to them. As she walked, her fat, fleshy thighs wobbled like two pink jellies. She had blond, almost white hair sticking out in all directions, like Pansy Potter in the *Beano*.

"Hello, Plimmys, you from London?"

"Yes," said Joyce. "Can you tell me where we find Mrs Godball."

"She's down there, in the door past the bike shed, but you're not allowed in till the bell goes."

"Oh," said Joyce. "I'll go anyway. Vee, you stay here."

The spiky-haired girl turned to Vee, bouncing her tennis ball as she spoke.

"You evacuees?"

"Yes, that's right."

"From London, aren't you?"

"Yes. Hackney."

"Oh, ah, thought so. You talk funny."

Vee thought that was a bit of a nerve considering her own Wiltshire twang.

"D'you want to play Two Balls?"

"O.K.," said Vee, pleased to have found a friend. The girl said her name was Doreen Noblock and her father owned the grocer's shop.

Wib walked over to the gang of boys playing picture cards in the corner. They took no notice of him at first. After a while the biggest boy looked up and scowled. He had bulbous frog's eyes and stared unpleasantly at Wib.

"Who are you?"

"I've just arrived. I'm from Hackney—London."

"What you come down here for? We don't like Londoners, they're dirty," said another boy, wearing a leather pilot's hat with ear flaps. "They've got all sorts of diseases."

"You ain't got nits, have you?" said a small boy with ears that stuck out like taxi doors.

"No," answered Wib, trying to keep his temper. He clutched his tin of cigarette cards a little tighter.

"Lice?"

"No."

"You don't wear vests, either. They wrap you up in brown paper—my mum told me."

"I've got a vest!" Wib protested.

"Why haven't you got no boots, Plimmy?"

Wib looked down at his dirty plimsolls and realised why they were calling him "Plimmy". He'd never owned a pair of boots or shoes in his life, but he wasn't letting on to this lot.

"Lost 'em in an air-raid."

Taxi Ears, Frog Eyes and Pilot Hat rolled around laughing. Wib started to get angry with these 'lippy' country boys.

"That's right, we got bombed out. You haven't even seen a bomb down here. You don't know what it's like. You don't know there's a war on, like the rest of us."

Taxi Ears stopped himself laughing to reply.

"That's where you're wrong, Plimmy. We had a German bomber crash just near here, the other side of Pottley. A Junkers 88 it was. We all got bits from it. It's still there—what's left of it. You never had a real live bomber crash near you, I bet."

Wib was a little shaken by this revelation. Amongst all the bombing and fires in Hackney it was true he'd never seen a crashed aeroplane. He changed the subject, turning his attention to the picture cards.

"What game are you playing? Topsies or Knock-downs?"

"It's none of your business," said Frog Eyes.

"You can't play, anyway," said Taxi Ears. "You've got no cards."

Wib rather smugly presented his tin and with great ceremony opened the lid to reveal his picture cards.

"All right," said Frog Eyes, "you can play. But no crying if you lose 'em. We play winner keepsies down here, right?"

"Right," confirmed Wib.

"Topsies," said Pilot Hat. "You go first."

Battle commenced and one by one Wib took them on. Each game followed the same pattern; he would lose a few to start with but the moment his special card of Mrs Johnson came into play, he would win the lot. By the time the teacher, Mrs Godball, rang the bell, Wib had cleaned out the three local boys completely. Understandably, they were far from pleased. Frog Eyes grabbed hold of the front of Wib's jersey.

"That card's a cheat card, Plimmy. Let me have a look at it. It's too thick. It's not a picture card at all."

Wib pulled away from him.

"Leave off, Frog Eyes, else I'll whack you."

Wib wasn't quite as brave as he pretended, but on first days at school you have to make an impression.

"Yeah, you and whose army, Plimmy?"

"I warn you three now, I've got a right hook like a sledge-hammer that could put you all in hospital."

The bluff worked because the three local boys backed off. Wib pulled his jumper straight, picked up his tin and walked away, rather pleased with himself. He was also pleased they hadn't taken him up on it because, to be honest, his right hook was more like a feather duster than a sledge-hammer.

There were only three classrooms at Pottley School and so Wib and Vee found themselves in the same class. Joyce was put into a small room with three other "seniors" and apart from the rare occasion when Mrs Godball popped her head in, they had to get on with lessons by themselves.

A big Government poster in Joyce's room said, "Be warned! Education is the first casualty of War." This amused Joyce who immediately imagined rows and rows of teachers with bandaged arms and broken legs.

Vee found her seat next to Doreen Noblock, who had been asked by Mrs Godball to look after her. Wib was put next to a boy who was even smaller than he was (and Wib was no giant). His name was Arthur Mortensen. On the other side of Wib sat a tubby boy with hair so short there was a gap of bare skin a good two inches above his ears. He was called Cyril Spicer and his father was the village barber, which accounted for his hair (or rather lack of it). Cyril's nick-name was 'Winnie', for the simple reason that he reminded Mrs Godball of the Prime Minister.

Fortunately for Wib, Frog Eyes, Taxi Ears and

Pilot Hat were at the far side of the class. Their real names were Gilbert Bootwick, Derek Fitch and Gordon Newman. All three scowled at him as he sat down.

As Mrs Godball droned on about Regularity, Punctuality, Industry and Obedience, Arthur Mortensen leaned over and whispered in Wib's ear.

"We're going mole-ing tonight. Coming?"

"What's mole-ing?" Wib whispered back, using his hand as a shield.

"Catching moles."

"But I don't know what a mole is."

He must have whispered too loud because Mrs Godball interrupted her chat about "doing right and fearing not" and threw him a dirty look. Arthur pushed a drawing across to Wib. It was of a funny-looking animal, a bit like a hairy mouse. Or maybe Arthur was just rotten at drawing.

"Catching moles. Down at Cuffley Elbow," said Arthur, for the last time.

Wib nodded agreement and smiled faintly. He had no idea what Cuffley Elbow was but he looked forward to seeing his first mole. Cyril Spicer grinned at Wib—obviously he was coming too.

Suddenly, to the astonishment of the whole class, a policeman had appeared at the door and was clearly visible through the glass panes.

Hands shot up all over the room to draw Mrs

Godball's attention to him. Doreen Noblock blurted it out first.

"Mrs G, Mrs G, there's Mr Keogh. I think he wants you."

Mrs Godball swung around to see Police Constable Keogh, who beckoned her outside.

"Carry on reading, children."

The whole class buzzed with speculation as to the reason for his visit, but no clue was given from the comic gestures of the two of them. Something had been stolen, somebody whispered.

Wib lifted up the lid of his desk and checked that his tin of picture cards was safe. He flicked through them till he saw the face of the young Mrs Johnson smiling up at him. Carefully, and with great affection, he stroked the edges before putting it back in the tin.

At the back of the class Gilbert Bootwick watched Wib's every move with his crafty, froggy eyes.

CHAPTER 12
DINGLE'S PIECE AND CUFFLEY ELBOW

Lunch at Mrs Bixey's was a delicious lamb stew, which filled them up so much they had a job running back to school. Wib, it had been decided, would have lunch with Mrs Bixey so as not to interrupt Miss Doughbridge's morning. This pleased Wib no end. At least he'd have one good meal a day.

Along Urchley Lane, they once more skipped up the bank to avoid the big puddles that seemed permanently in their way. Would they ever go away? wondered Vee. Or were they always there as an obstacle that had to be overcome?

Mrs Godball's strong wrists shook the hand-bell rigorously, denoting the beginning of after-noon lessons. The children noisily filed into the crowded classroom and squeezed behind their desks. Vee discussed the finer points of her lamb stew with Doreen Noblock, who was really more interested in a complicated cats cradle she was playing with Enid Skinner. Mrs Godball clapped her hands.

"Quiet now, children. Break's over. Older group, get out No. 2 English Reader; younger group, get out your green exercise books.

There was a noise like machine-gun fire as the

desk lids banged open. Wib caught a lump in his throat as he looked inside his desk. The tin of picture cards had been spilled out all over his books and there, on top of the rest, was the 'special' of Mrs Johnson. The only difference was that it had been torn into little pieces. He tried to put them together, but it was hopeless.

"Anything wrong, Harris?" said Mrs Godball, noticing that he was the last to get his book out.

"No, miss," Wib managed to say. The tears were beginning to form in his eyes, but he was determined not to cry. Over in the other corner Frog Eyes and Taxi Ears were sniggering uncontrollably behind their No. 2 English Readers.

After school, Joyce left Vee and Wib to go their different ways with their new friends. Wib was off mole-ing with Cyril and Arthur at Cuffley Elbow, and Vee had vanished to a "secret place" Doreen and Enid had found near Dingle's Piece.

Joyce had promised to send the postcard they'd been given the moment they'd arrived, and Mrs Godball had kindly let her stay behind to write it. She had always been good at composition at school but had never had to write a letter or card before. What should she say? How they hated it? But they didn't really—except for Miss Doughbridge. Joyce chewed the end of her pen and stared at a map of the British Empire on the wall. England looked so small it made Wiltshire seem like it was next door to London. But right now it didn't feel like it at all. She dipped her nib into the white china ink-well and began to write.

"Dear Mum,
Here we are safe and sound, not in Bath as we thought but near a place called Devizes which they say is in Wiltshire, right in the country. We have been sent to a village called Pottley. I think that's how you spell it and we have been put with a nice man and lady called Mr and Mrs Bixey in a farm, with cows, chickens and smashing fields and sheep and things. The address is Butt's Farm, Urchley Lane, Pottley, Wiltshire. Wib is not with us but don't be angry because he is not very far away, only next door really at the house of a lady called Miss Doughbridge who also owns the house where Vee and me are . . ."

Joyce was running out of room on the post-card so she couldn't say any more, even if she knew how.

". . . that's all for now. Love to Freddy and Siddy and you of course. Vee and Wib send lots of kisses, please write soon.
Love Joyce."

On the right hand side she wrote down the address, c/o The Hare and Hounds and Uncle Stanley. She threw her coat over her shoulders and hurried to catch the post. Mrs Bixey had promised to show her how to make homemade bread if she got home early.

Vee, Enid and Doreen ran down Sloops Alley, in between Spicer's barber shop and Old Porch Cottage. The narrow alley led to the Mission Hall, behind which was a wide-open green slope that led up to a hill called Dingle's Piece. As they walked, Doreen told Vee of their "secret place". At the bottom of Dingle's Piece the fields dropped away, and tucked into the hillside was a small-holding called Black Dog Farm. Old Mr Critchley who used to own the farm had died last January and the place had been left untouched. His wife had died only six months before him and Mrs Noblock, Doreen's mother, had said it was probably a broken heart.

"What about the animals?" Vee asked.

"Oh, they soon went—escaped or got pinched most of 'em," said Doreen. "My dad had a couple of his hens—everybody did. But nobody touched the house."

"It's too scary anyway," Enid piped in. "Everything's as he left it—there's even his dinner on the table."

Doreen continued.

"And there's a dip in his bed where he was lying before he dropped off."

"Dropped off?" asked Vee.

"Snuffed it, passed away, dead," said Enid, in a matter of fact way.

They climbed over a broken wall that had been neglected for some long time. Vee had to be careful not to catch her coat on a length of barbed wire.

"How d'you know all this?"

"'Cause we looked through the window—we haven't been inside, it's too scary."

At the bottom of the hill Vee could see the small house and out-buildings of Black Dog Farm.

"You sure there's no one here?" she said, a little warily.

"No one at all—except ghosts, that is!" Doreen and Enid laughed out loud and Vee joined in. Doreen put her finger to her lips.

"Ssh! Just in case . . ." she whispered.

The three of them slowly and silently crept up to the lonely-looking, single-storey farmhouse.

At Cuffley Elbow, Arthur Mortensen and Cyril Spicer showed Wib the finer arts of mole-ing. First they looked for the tell-tale piles of earth the moles had thrown up whilst burrowing into the ground. Arthur opened the neck of the sack he was carrying and took out a metal trap; he clicked it open and pushed it into the soft earth with his toe. He then moved on to another pile of earth and repeated the process. Wib began to wonder how big a mole was. The nasty-looking trap seemed capable of catching a small lion at the very least.

"Right, that's it," said Arthur 'The Mole' Mortensen. "We'll come back and see how they're getting on a bit later. Now we'll show you the locks and the canal."

Wib was pleased at the prospect of seeing the canal. It reminded him of Eagle Wharf, Hackney; and home. Cyril Spicer took a great chunk of treacle toffee from his pocket and snapped off pieces for Wib and Arthur.

"Where d'you get this?" said Wib, unaccustomed to such luxuries.

"Me mum makes it, best there is. She won a prize once at Devizes Fair for best treacle toffee in the county. Keep chewing mind, else it sticks your teeth together."

Wib bit into the black gooey toffee and made his jaws ache keeping it on the go—he didn't want his mouth to be sealed forever. A lot of people might have thought that an advantage, but Wib didn't.

There was a cold breeze cutting through Cuffley Elbow which pinched Wib's nose and made him button his coat. But through the trees he could see the hard sunlight glinting on the still water of the canal. This warmed him up no end.

Wib's pleasure, however, was short-lived when they reached the second lock gate. Further down the canal bank he could see "Frog Eyes" Gilbert Bootwick. He and his two companions had crept along the thick wooden sluice gates and were perched in the middle, fishing with homemade bamboo rods.

Wib, Cyril and Arthur ducked down out of sight. On a grass verge Wib could see three bicycles, nearer to him than their owners. He had no doubt who had torn up his picture card of Mrs Johnson, and he was determined to get his own back.

Slowly he crept along on his stomach towards the bicycles. He had a plan.

Vee, Doreen and Enid had reached the window of Black Dog Farm. Doreen gradually eased herself up to peep inside.

"Look, Vee, this was his bedroom."

Vee peered through the dirty glass. Enid and Doreen hadn't been exaggerating; it certainly was a strange sight. The bedroom was cluttered with Old Critchley's personal bits and pieces; photographs, even his false teeth in a glass at the side of his bed. But the bed itself was the eeriest thing of all; you could see by the dip in the bedclothes that he had been lying there before he died. You could even see where his head had rested on the pillow.

At the side of the house a door was slightly ajar. Slowly, Doreen and Enid crept inside. Vee held back.

"Come on, Vee," hissed Doreen.

"Supposing someone comes."

"No one lives here, silly."

"Why are you going inside then?"

"'Cause we want to show you how he left his dinner before he died."

Doreen took Vee by the hand and the three girls tip-toed into the kitchen.

"Look, there it is, see . . ." Doreen's eyes nearly popped out of her head. There was indeed a meal on the table, but it wasn't Old Critchley's—because he'd been dead for eight months now and this dinner was still steaming hot.

"Someone must be here," whispered Doreen.

Just then, in the living room across the hall, they heard someone fiddling with the tuner knob on a crackling radio. Needless to say, they didn't stop to see who it was. Doreen was out of the back door first, closely followed by Vee and Enid. The three of them ran for all they were worth across the farmyard and over the stone wall. Vee ran faster than all of them. Not just because she was a better runner, but because, as she left the kitchen, she had seen something that Enid and Doreen hadn't. On the chair by the gas stove was a soldier's uniform. And lying on top of that was a white stick and blind man's glasses. The dinner on the table belonged to Old Stoopy, the man they had spotted on the train.

Wib had finally crawled up to where Gilbert Bootwick's bicycle was lying on the canal bank. It was a shiny, new black Hudson and the saddle-bag was now practically by Wib's hand. Gingerly he undid the buckles and saw what he'd hoped to find: a small tool kit. He opened it up and took out the spanner.

Arthur and Cyril watched from a safe distance. They knew Gilbert Bootwick of old and had learned to steer clear of him and his cronies at all times. Gilbert's father was a big, brash man whose loud mouth and aggressive manner made him generally disliked by the rest of the villagers. Bullying Gilbert was a chip off the old block.

Wib slowly unscrewed the nuts that gripped the wheels to the front forks of the bicycle, and then systematically undid the chain and any other spare nut or bolt he could see.

Cyril and Arthur watched Wib with complete admiration.

"He must be mad, what's he doing?"

"Search me."

Out in the middle of the canal Gilbert's frog eyes were firmly set on his fishing float, as it bobbed around on the surface of the water. His two companions, one on either side of him, were also concentrating on their fishing, and on keeping their balance on the sluice gate.

Wib crawled along for as far as the long grass gave him cover. Then, quite boldly, he stood up and ran towards the lock.

"He really is mad!" whispered Cyril to Arthur.

Before Gilbert and Co. spotted him, Wib

had reached the long arm that opened the gates. With all his strength he pushed the wooden tiller, clanking the metal cogs into action, and gradually the gates parted. Frog Eyes and friends watched unmoving, almost as surprised as Cyril and Arthur. They were sitting on the half of the gate nearest the far bank and consequently, as the gap in the middle got wider, were marooned. Safe in the knowledge that they couldn't reach him, Wib ran back to the bicycles. He picked up the two that he hadn't tampered with and rolled them down the grass verge. They hit the concrete edge and bounced high before splashing into the water. Gilbert Bootwick shook his fist at Wib.

"You'll be for it, Plimmy, when we fish them out."

"Oh yeah?" shouted Wib. "You will, will you?"

Wib picked up Frog Eyes' own bicycle and, with great show, rolled it down the bank. As it hit the concrete, Gilbert's eyes bulged even more. Certainly the bike bounced up in the air in one piece, but the impact shook the machine so vigorously that it descended into the water in twenty different parts.

"Fish that one out, Frog Eyes," Wib shouted in defiance. Arthur and Cyril were clutching their sides with laughter, but wisely kept their heads down. After all, they wouldn't want Frog Eyes to think they were in on it—he had a long memory.

Wib casually walked away whistling

"Umbrella Man" as loudly as his puffed up cheeks would allow.

"Come on, Arthur, let's see about those moles."

CHAPTER 13
BOOTS

For Wib, the next few weeks were made up of wonderful days crammed full of exploration and discovery. Days of mole-ing and bird-nesting with Cyril and Arthur at Cuffley Elbow, pirates on the canal, and cowboys and indians at Oven Bottom. Days of Germans and Frenchies over the old chain bridge; days of cavaliers and roundheads at Cromwell's Camp near Nubbley Edge. And cops and robbers (keeping an eye on Old Stoopy, the army deserter) at Black Dog Farm.

On the other hand, his nights were miserable. Miss Doughbridge had for too long lost the joy out of her own life to be able to bring any to one small boy. She saw good in nothing and Wib saw adventure in everything. Miss Liggerty was worse because Miss Doughbridge chastised her and treated her like an old house-cloth; and so she took it out on Wib. He would be made to eat his evening meal alone in the dining room, at the end of an enormous table that had twelve place-settings. The room was cheerless and cold and however shiny the table top and sparkling the cutlery, the food was rotten and the welcome unfriendly.

Miss Liggerty would put his plate down in front of him and stay just long enough to say grace and tell him which knife and fork to use; then she would close the door, leaving him to eat alone. Around the table were eleven empty chairs, and it didn't help any to think of them occupied by eleven ghostly companions. Wib would shake his head to get rid of such notions.

The food he was given was cold, tasteless and there was never enough of it. Over the unlit fireplace was a large clock; its tick seemed to get louder as Wib got lonelier. If only Freddy was here, however miserable the surroundings, at least there would be someone to giggle with when the short-sighted Miss Liggerty bumped into the table. Somehow it wasn't so funny on your own.

Wib also hated Miss Doughbridge's cats. They were called Cane and Abel, which was apt because one was given an inordinate amount of affection whilst the other was kicked at regular intervals. They would hiss and snarl whenever Wib passed, and stared at him with a vicious, superior look that they must have learned from their mistress.

Wib had got into the habit of filling himself up with second portions of Mrs Bixey's lunch, so a rotten evening meal worried him little. But at night he could do nothing about the loneliness of his gas-lit bedroom.

He would lie awake for hours thinking of the pleasures and expeditions of the day, listening to the hiss of the gas mantle and staring at the religious pictures. The memory of the angels with outstretched hands and the feeling of continual coldness would stay with him for the rest of his life.

Vee and Joyce were luckier. Mrs Bixey was kind and generous, with more recipes for homemade dishes than ever the girls could have dreamed of. In contrast to Wib, their room was cosy and warm and instead of prayers last thing at night, Mrs Bixey would provide them with a hot cup of cocoa, which they would nurse for hours to avoid having to go off to bed. Mr Bixey tended to go down to the George & Dragon a lot and arrived back nearly drunk most nights and very drunk on Saturday nights.

One evening he had more than one too many and lost the key to the shed in which they stored the precious farm petrol. Miss Doughbridge had received the Government allowance for the three farms she owned and it had been safely locked up, in jerry-cans, in the shed. Joyce and Vee cried with laughter as they watched Mr Bixey scrambling around blind drunk in the farmyard mud, until he found the key. From that day onwards he always kept it safely attached to the end of his watch-chain.

Vee had formed a firm friendship with Doreen Noblock and, like Wib, she had been shown every secret copse and gully in Pottley. The two of them would pick bunches of wild flowers in the lanes and Mrs Gubber at Frogshitch Farm let them collect the eggs from the chicken runs. Vee could never believe that they were still warm. There was "Tarzans" at Castleford Farm where there was a barn with long ropes that you could swing on and yell like the "King of the Jungle". There was "Stowaways" amongst the empty ale casks behind the George & Dragon, which left your clothes smelling of best bitter.

Mrs Noblock had also taken a liking to Vee and would let her stay late, playing dozens of games of Happy Families and drinking mugs of rather weak cocoa. It wasn't nearly as nice as Mrs Bixey's evening drink, but Doreen's company more than made up for it.

Joyce had even been allowed to go to a dance at the Mission Hall in aid of the "Spitfire and Comfort Fund". Mrs Townsend, the undertaker's wife, had organised it and she spent the whole evening bullying people into dancing to the awful three-piece band, imported from Urchley Marshes.

Joyce had never been to a dance before and the whole thing was a lovely, if somewhat frightening, experience. She wore one of Mrs Bixey's old frocks, that she had long since grown out of. Best of all, Eric Spicer, Cyril's rather spotty, but kindly, elder brother, had asked her to do the Gay Gordons which she'd never even heard of, let alone danced. Then everybody joined in a waltz and sang aloud the Vera Lynn song "See The Pyramids Along The Nile"; Joyce pretended to know the words. Eric had even had the nerve to ask her if he could walk her home down Urchley Lane. She had shyly said no, but by way of consolation agreed to borrow his umbrella, as it was raining rather heavily. She'd already arranged to meet Mr Bixey outside the George & Dragon at half-past ten and he would take her home. As it turned out, Mr Bixey was so drunk it was Joyce who took *him* home.

Three weeks had flown by and all three Harris children had settled into country life with so much ease that they wondered why they had ever had any doubts.

Miss Doughbridge rarely left Butt's House. Mr Bixey said it was a "proper" nervous disease that he'd read about in Pear's Encyclopaedia—"being as she was frightened of crowds." She even held her own church service every Sunday in her front parlour, to avoid going to St Mary's. Miss Liggerty would accompany the hymns on a small pump organ and Miss Doughbridge's two cats—Cane and Abel—would complete the tiny congregation.

On the first Monday in every month, they would go into Devizes to visit Miss Doughbridge's step-sister at the mental hospital.

"We're going to visit relations at the rest home," she would say, but all the children knew she was going to the loony bin.

It was after one such visit that Miss Doughbridge returned with some unexpected gifts.

She called the three of them into her hall and there, neatly laid out on the polished lino, were three pairs of black leather boots. Miss Doughbridge instructed them to thank her for the generous gift and also to thank Miss Liggerty for sparing the time to go to Herberts, the bootmakers, to fetch them. Vee, as always, immediately turned up her nose. Joyce wondered if Eric Spicer would ever ask her to do the Gay Gordons again if she wore these clumsy clodhoppers to another Spitfire and Comfort Fund dance.

On the other hand, Wib was delighted with his new footwear. The metal studs on the soles meant he could slide fifteen feet or more in the school playground. Something he could never do in plimsolls.

Going home that evening Wib, Joyce and Vee came across the inevitable puddle that stretched across the full width of Urchley Lane. Instead of skipping around the edge, as they had learned to do, Wib strolled right through the middle in his new leather boots. Joyce and Vee started to laugh and then joined him in the puddle. Wib splashed around like Jack Hulbert and Joyce and Vee laughed even more, which they shouldn't have done because it only encouraged him. With an enormous jump he leapt up in the air and landed six inches away from Vee, causing the water to flood over her feet and down the tops of her boots. She stopped laughing just long enough to do the same to Wib—except it splashed as high as his coat. In seconds the three of them were wildly jumping around in the deep puddle, as if it was a paddling pond in the local park. Very soon they were drenched from head to toe and their boots were squelching and sodden from the water.

"We'll be for it if Miss Doughbridge sees us," said Vee.

"Don't worry," Wib answered. "She'll be having her afternoon nap—she won't see us."

Wib was wrong, because Miss Doughbridge had been watching the entire performance through a large pair of binoculars which she often used to check on intruders to Oven Bottom and Butt's Field. She was waiting for them as they walked through the gate.

"William, take off your boots at the door and then remove yourself to bed immediately."

"But it's still light, miss," protested Wib.

"Bed. Immediately."

"He didn't mean nothing, miss," offered Joyce, in an attempt to placate her.

"Be quiet, girl. How dare you tell me what he meant and what he didn't mean. I saw the whole thing with my own eyes."

"But we were to blame too, miss."

"You *were* indeed and you too will be going straight to bed. I have instructed Mrs Bixey on no account to give you an evening meal. Is that clear?"

Wib didn't bother to answer; he just squelched off to his room.

In the Bixey's house Joyce and Vee pulled off their boots in total silence. Handing them a towel, Mrs Bixey gave them a slight smile which meant they were forgiven—well, nearly. More importantly, it also meant that they were sure of a mug of hot soup, at the very least.

As always, Wib wasn't so lucky. His room was as cold and damp as ever. His teeth started to chatter as he wrung out his clothes and laid them over the chair. He slipped into his plimsolls which felt friendly and much more comfortable than the boots he was beginning to hate.

He dried his legs on the curtain that covered a small alcove in the corner of the room. It made a squeaking noise as the rusty curtain-rings scraped along the metal rail.

It was the kind of noise that puts your teeth on edge, and Wib winced. He thought it would be a good Chinese torture to tie Miss Liggerty up and make the curtains screech over and over again, until she went mad and had to be sent to the looney bin.

The idea made Wib laugh and his teeth stopped chattering for a bit. It was then that he noticed a crack in the plaster at the back of the alcove. Not that there was anything special about a crack, there were hundreds all over the old house. But this crack was perfectly straight and traced out an area about five feet square. Wib moved closer to get a better look.

His curiosity made him forget his wet clothes. Tapping the square, he found that it was not plaster like the rest of the wall, but plywood. He managed to squeeze the tips of his fingers into the part where the crack was widest. Without a thought for Miss Doughbridge's interior decor, he yanked the piece of plywood clean off the wall and landed upside down on the lino, covered in bits of plaster and splintered wood. He then made a very important discovery.

As the cloud of dust cleared he saw that the plywood had been deliberately put there to cover up a small door. It had no handle—although there was a hole that probably once held a knob. His mind quickly speculated upon every possibility of the cupboard's contents. Dead bodies? Hidden treasure? Black market tea? Or perhaps even counterfeit ten bob notes? With great excitement he put his finger in the hole and tugged at the door.

The door opened quite smoothly. The first thing Wib noticed was that it had to be more than a cupboard, because there were no shelves or hooks, just blackness. Suddenly, he heard Miss Liggerty on the landing outside his bedroom.

"William, are you asleep?" she called out in her whining voice.

"Er, no, miss . . . not yet."

Wib leapt out of the alcove and pulled the curtain across. He swept the loose plaster and splinters under the bed with the side of his foot, and with one leap was under the feather eiderdown. Miss Liggerty's hand rattled the door handle.

"What have you done with your wet clothes?"

"It's all right, miss, I'm decent."

The door opened a little wider and Miss Liggerty popped her head round. Wib couldn't see the rest of her body—it looked quite eerie to see a disembodied head seemingly floating by itself in the darkness. Miss Liggerty's long, scraggy, rubber neck allowed her to perform such miracles of contortion.

"What, miss?"

"Pardon, miss." Miss Liggerty corrected him.

"Pardon, miss?"

"What have you done with your wet clothes? You're not sleeping in them, are you?"

"No, miss. I'm kipping in my vest, it didn't get wet. The rest of my clobber's hanging over the chair."

He nodded towards the clothes and Miss Liggerty came into the room to collect them. She walked past the curtain that hid his secret door. Wib bit his lip in case she discovered it. Miss Liggerty picked up the clothes and moved away, tripping over something as she went. It was a piece of plaster from the wall.

"What's this?"

Wib's brain raced to think of an answer.

"Er, chalk, miss . . . for the hop-scotch in the playground."

Luckily Miss Liggerty accepted his explanation. She placed the plaster on the chest of drawers.

"Don't leave it lying on the floor, please. Things under foot should not be put. It's a saying you might well remember."

"Yes, miss. I like your sayings. Proper clever they are."

"Goodnight."

"Goodnight, miss. Sorry about the boots, we got a bit carried away."

Miss Liggerty was a little taken aback by his politeness.

"The recognition of sin is the beginning of salvation, William. You might remember that also."

"Yes, miss. 'Night."

Miss Liggerty had no sooner closed the door than Wib was out of bed and into the alcove. He took the box of Swan Vestas from his picture card tin and struck a match. The glow was enough for him to confirm that it was no cupboard he had discovered—it was a passage. Slowly he edged forward. It wasn't really a secret passageway because, now he was inside, he could see a china sink and shelves, filled with bed pans and chamber pots. Everything was coated in layers of dust and joined together by thick cobwebs. It was clear no one had been in Wib's passage for a very long time, probably even before Miss Doughbridge lived there—if you could think that far back. Wib looked for another exit.

"Ouch!" he yelped as the match came to an end and burned his fingers. He didn't much like the idea of being in the dark. He fumbled for a new match as the cobwebs stroked his face like the fingers of a friendly ghost. Bursting into flame, the match lit up the other end of the passageway.

Sure enough there was another door and on the other side he could hear muffled voices. Wib crept a little closer but there was no mistaking who it was: Miss Doughbridge was shouting as usual at Miss Liggerty, who whined excuses.

To the right of the door Wib could see a narrow wooden staircase. Gently and silently, he tip-toed down the stairs as they cork-screwed into darkness.

At the bottom he came to what looked like a dead end. If it was a door it wouldn't budge; he brushed his hand over the surface of the wood and felt a key. There was a crisp 'click' and the door opened inwards. Wib's match was blown out by the gush of cold wind that suddenly rushed in. He peered out into the moonlight.

To his great delight, he discovered that the door led out into the field at the side of Butt's House and was completely hidden by thick branches of the wisteria tree that clutched the wall.

Wib couldn't believe his luck. He ran back up the narrow stairs, not even needing a light. Taking the big fluffy eiderdown from his bed, he wrapped it over his shoulders and returned to the passageway.

Once out into the field Wib ran about like an escaped lunatic, tasting his new found freedom. He didn't even care if Miss Doughbridge was looking out through her binoculars—although she'd certainly get a shock if she saw this mad eiderdown with legs cavorting around in her field.

Suddenly Wib stopped dead in his tracks. He could hear noises. He climbed over the stone wall, clinging on to his makeshift coat as best he could, and looked down into Hawk's Field.

There were two men chasing the Hawk's Farm sheep around the field. Wib laughed quietly to himself as they lunged at the bleating animals with crude rugby tackles. His smile quickly vanished though when one of the men caught up with a slower sheep. He brutally pulled its legs out sideways, sat astride its back and, with a large rock, proceeded to pound the poor animal senseless. Wib was horrified and, without thinking, ran towards the two men, screaming.

Looking up from the bloody carcass, the two sheep thieves stared at the apparition as it ran towards them. They couldn't see Wib's head because it was covered with the eiderdown, which billowed outwards in the wind like a mediaeval cape. He clutched it to him and waved with his free arm.

"Bloody hell, what's that?" said the man with the rock in his hand.

"It's a demon. Look, it's got no head."

Wib's short white legs poked out of the eiderdown and, aided by the subtle tricks of moonlight, he looked quite frightening. The men were in two minds what to do.

"It's Squill!"

"Who?"

"The one-armed ghost."

"Ghost?"

"Of Sir Percival Squill."

"Don't be bloody daft, there's no such thing!"

"No?"

They decided to take no chances. When Wib got within ten yards of them the two men scampered off. Reaching the body of the lifeless sheep, he stopped running and screwed up his eyes to get a better look at the thieves. He could have been mistaken in the half light, but the second man seemed to be leaning forward as he scuttled away. Just like Old Stoopy.

CHAPTER 14
FREDDY

"Freddy's coming, Wib!" were the first words Wib heard the next morning as he met Joyce and Vee in the yard.

"He's coming on the train."

"He's out of hospital."

"His ears are O.K.—well, sort of."

Joyce and Vee tripped over one another in their enthusiasm to give Wib the news first.

"He's been evacuated."

"Where to?"

Wib got his question in quickly, half expecting a rotten answer like "Scotland"; or somewhere even further like Canada.

"*Here*, stupid!" said Joyce.

"With *you*? With the Bixey's?"

"No, with *you*—Drawbridge is getting Old Liggerty to look after both of you."

"When?"

"Guess."

"I can't guess."

"Today!"

"You're kidding me."

"We're not. It's true, look read Mum's postcard."

Wib took the postcard and read every line over and over again. Each time his smile got wider, until it had plainly spread from ear to ear.

"He's going to stay here with me!" Wib told Joyce, as if he was giving *them* the news.

"That's what we told you! You daft 'appath. Mr Bixey's taking us into Devizes at eleven o'clock to meet him." Wib was convinced and ran off down the lane waving the postcard.

Arthur Mortensen and Cyril Spicer were probably the best mates you could have, but somehow it wasn't the same as a proper brother. Most important of all, he would have someone to share his lonely room at night. His eyes sparkled mischievously at the thought. The sounds of the two of them giggling would liven up the coldest, dampest room.

The bus ride to Devizes was a pleasure in itself—there was a lovely feeling of going back over the journey they had originally made as strangers. Now, only one month later, they were fully-fledged country children.

They passed the one-armed statue of Sir Percival Squill who somehow didn't look at all frightening now. It prompted Wib to tell his sisters about his adventures and discoveries of the previous night. News of Freddy's arrival had pushed them right out of his mind. His description of the eiderdown over his head and Old Stoopy running off into the night made Joyce and Vee roar with laughter. Naturally they didn't believe a word of it. Mr Bixey picked up his ears.

"Sheep stealing? Did I hear you say sheep-stealing?"

"No, Mr Bixey," Wib said quickly. "We're talking about the rustler in the Gene Autrey film we saw at the Palace."

Mr Bixey went back to his newspaper. An advertisement for Bodyguard Soap featuring evacuees had caught his eye. It said, "We're fifteen in the house now, not counting the germs." Above it an advertisement for S.R. Toothpaste had the simple headline: "For Gum-Rot." Mr Bixey touched his teeth with his tongue. They were still there.

They passed Torney End Farm where the two Kennedy children had been billeted. The sign that once said "Trespassers Will Be Prosecuted", now read "Trespassers except postmen will be boiled alive in oil"—a sure indication that the Londoners were making their presence felt.

Devizes was a hubbub of people on a Saturday morning and, but for the "Oh, ahs" and "Aah, ees" of the Wiltshire accents floating past, it could almost have been London. The streets and alleyways intrigued Vee no end and she read the names aloud as they passed: Monday Market Street, The Brittox, Snuffs Alley. Joyce was more interested in the shops: Bon Ton High Class Confectioners, Madame Maureen's Underwear de Paris, Herberts the Bootmakers; there was even a Woolworths like the one in Hackney.

The Palace cinema announced: "Deanna Durbin delights cinema-goers this week with *It's A Date*." Joyce wondered if Cyril Spicer's spotty brother Eric might take her.

Down Station Road there was a fire practice at the old Corn Exchange. A large crowd had gathered to watch as the firemen trained their hoses on a make-believe blaze. Wib edged up to a local boy standing on the edge of the crowd.

"Practising are they?"

"Oh, ah," replied the local, without taking his eyes off the gushing water.

"In case there's a real fire?" Wib asked.

"Oh, ah."

"Typical—that's about as near as you lot will get to the bloody real war, mate."

"Oh, ah." The small boy took his eyes off the water for a moment to watch Wib walking away. Wib had a very superior look on his face.

The narrow platform at Devizes Station was crowded with people waiting for the London train. Mr Bixey sat on a green wooden bench, next to a fat lady wearing indoor carpet slippers with a pom-pom. She rested her foot on her knee and rubbed it.

"Feet playing me up rotten, they are."

Mr Bixey nodded politely but carried on reading his *Wiltshire Gazette*.

"Carbuncles. That's what they are. D'you hear me? Carbuncles!"

"Nasty," said Mr Bixey.

"*Bloody* nasty. They your kids?" inquired the fat lady, pointing to Joyce and Vee.

"No. They're staying with us—evacuees. From London."

"I'm from London. Cross Street, Islington. Know it?"

"No, 'fraid not."

"I hate the bleedin' country. The birds and the chickens keep me awake in the morning. The Woolworths is smaller than our corner shop, the bus service is worse than useless and all the free fruit's given me diarrhoea."

Mr Bixey once more smiled politely. This time he ventured into conversation.

"Oh, it's not so bad here. Away from the bombs."

The woman carried on as if she hadn't heard him.

"And they don't want us here, the locals. Stuck up bleeders. Every time something gets nicked it's us lot who gets blamed—my boys are always being dragged down the nick—sometimes for pinching hardly anything at all."

Mr Bixey ignored her this time; coincidentally he had noticed a headline in his paper that said, "Epidemic of Petty Theft—Evacuees Blamed."

Joyce looked expectantly along the empty railroad tracks, waiting for Freddy's train. She thought she had seen a puff of smoke in the distance, but it had disappeared behind a hill.

Wib and Joyce looked at the advertising posters that had been neatly pasted across the station walls. One said, ''Hop Into A Lifebuoy Toilet Soap Bath'' and showed a lady with no clothes on, which amused Wib. Underneath was the slogan ''Hard on B.O. Kind on the Skin.''

''What's B.O., Vee? Does it mean Buzz Off?''

''I don't know what it is—but it's not very nice.''

''Why?''

'''Cause people turn their noses up at you.''

''Why should they do that?''

Vee shrugged her shoulders.

''I don't know, but they do. I think it's a bit like nits—only ladies get it.''

The black steam train pulled into the station and thirty doors seemed to open simultaneously as mothers and children poured out. Very soon the platform was a busy mixture of hugging people, smiles, tears and steam.

It was through the steam that Freddy made his entrance. He looked almost like a character in a scene out of one of the war-time films at the Palace. He had a white bandage around his head and looked every inch the returning hero. Except, instead of khaki, he wore the evacuees uniform; navy blue mac, school cap, label, gas-mask, pillow-case, grey crumpled socks and . . . new sandals. New sandals! At least Freddy would be spared the great black 'clodhoppers' the other three were forced to wear. Joyce hugged him and Vee hugged both of them. Wib stood back until they had finished their silly girl stuff; then, with a nonchalant wave of the hand, he greeted his brother.

"Wotcha, Fred, got new sandals, I see."

"Yeah. Uncle Stanley bought 'em. I lost me plimsolls in the hospital."

Mr Bixey had taken off his hat and was ready to say hello, so Joyce introduced him.

"Freddy, this here is Mr Bixey who looks after Vee and me."

"How do, young 'un. Welcome to Devizes."

Joyce explained to Freddy, who was a little bewildered by all the commotion around him.

"You're going in with Wib at Miss Doughbridge's house. She's . . ." She glanced at Mr Bixey whose attention had been diverted by the fat lady with the carbuncles. Wib quickly finished Joyce's sentence.

". . . she's horrible. Old Drawbridge's got no face and Miss Liggerty's the lady who looks after us and she's got eyes like bloody whelks and the dinner's are muck and it's cold at night . . . but . . . you'll like the fields and things . . ."

Wib noticed that Mr Bixey had rejoined them after being introduced to the carbuncle lady's grand-daughter.

"Come on, young 'un. Let's get you to your new home—we've got a bus to catch."

"Their buses are single-decker with no stairs," Wib added, behind his hand, but Freddy had already been ushered off by Mr Bixey.

Freddy would have liked to get to sleep that night. London to Wiltshire was a long journey, but every time his eyes closed his brother would have another story to tell him.

There was Old Stoopy at Black Dog Farm; secret staircases; Cuffley Elbow; Oven Bottom; canals; locks; sheep thieves; Jip the dog; Arthur Mortensen's moles; Cyril Spicer's barber shop; the garden full of coffins; Gilbert "Frog Eyes" Bootwick; even Doreen Noblock sounded interesting. Freddy was beginning to like the idea of being an evacuee.

After one last look at the staircase, Wib turned out the gas and pitched the room into darkness. Freddy hadn't liked the look of "Whelk Eyes" Miss Liggerty and the faceless Miss Doughbridge frightened the life out of him, but otherwise he couldn't wait for morning to come and for Wib to show him the many wonders of Pottley village.

The light had been out for about two minutes when suddenly Freddy shook Wib awake.

"Wib, I forgot to tell you. They found Darkie! He's in a dog's home in Greenwich."

"That's good," murmured Wib, half asleep. "I hope he gets better dinners than we do!"

CHAPTER 15
THE STRAP

Freddy never wet the bed at Pottley. Wib told him that Miss Doughbridge would get another three-and-sixpence a week allowance if he did and it proved to be enough of a deterrent.

Wib was a good guide and Freddy soon got to know Pottley. Arthur and Cyril took to him in the same way as they had to Wib. And, much to Vee's annoyance, Doreen Noblock had also taken a liking to the quiet, gentle ways of her young brother.

Joyce, although the eldest, was probably the one who had fitted in the least to life at Pottley. There were no girls her age living nearby and she had grown out of the things that filled Vee, Wib and Freddy with so much pleasure.

She had taken to going to the cinema in Devizes twice a week and sometimes Eric Spicer would go along with her. He was a kind, if somewhat gormless lad, who had shot up rather too quickly in the last two years, with the consequence that he was six feet tall but his clothes were still only five foot six. His new height made him a little self-conscious and he would permanently lean his chin on his chest, as tall people often do, to make himself appear shorter.

Also he never did seem to be able to shake off

his rash of adolescent spots, which made him even less anxious to show himself in public. This made it very difficult for Joyce to persuade him to visit the pictures as often as she did.

Joyce saw everything the Palace had to offer. Rita Hayworth in *Circus Shadow*, *Shipyard Sally* with Gracie Fields, *Jack The Boy* with Cicely Courtneidge, and so many more. On her own, in her frock and plimsolls, she could get in half-price for eight pence. But when Eric could be persuaded to leave the safety of his father's barber shop she would pretend to be much older and fork out one-and-twopence, which she earned making shortcrust pastry for Mrs Bixey.

By way of a change, Eric had even once persuaded her to visit the Devizes Museum in Long Street. But Joyce found that the remains of ancient Britons didn't really compare with Greer Garson at the Palace.

To make amends, Eric had taken her for a cup of tea and a cup-cake at Strong's Tea Rooms. Unfortunately the cake tasted like cardboard and she upset spotty Eric by telling him so.

Whilst queueing up one night for Loretta Young in *Kentucky*, she noticed a small hand-written sign by the side of the advertising poster. It said: "Wanted. Part-time Usherettes. Apply Dennis Austin, Manager." It was the ideal solution—pictures without paying.

She nudged Eric.

"Look, Eric. They want part-time usherettes."

"I've got a job."

"Not you, Eric. Me!"

"That'll be nice."

"That means I'll be able to get into the pictures for free—buckshee!"

"That'll be nice." (Eric was a boy of very few words.)

"Then you won't have to keep taking me."

"That'll be nice."

"You'll be able to stay at home and clean your dad's lather bowls."

Eric thought for a while and then decided to say nothing. If there was one thing he hated more than Loretta Young, it was cleaning his dad's lather bowls.

Freddy was a little reluctant to visit Black Dog Farm. It wasn't so much that it reminded him of Darkie, but the picture Vee and Wib had painted of Old Stoopy and the spooky dead house had rather frightened him off.

His favourite place was the pigs' pen at Frogshitch Farm. He and Wib would spend hours leaning on the wall, watching the disgusting antics of the fat, dirty-looking animals. Compared to them, Freddy and Wib felt quite good-mannered. On the other hand, the poor pigs' dinners didn't look much worse than the ones Miss Liggerty put in front of them.

Doreen, Enid and Vee joined the boys in the barn. They had been to listen to the trains in

Stubbs Tunnel. There was a place, which only Enid knew, where if you put your ear to the ground you could hear the trains underneath as they thundered through the tunnel, cut deep into the hillside.

The girls giggled as Wib attempted to feed one of the porkers a cabbage on the end of a stick. Suddenly Joyce ran into the barn, looking distraught.

"Wib, come quick, they want you back at the house."

"Who do?" asked Wib. The pig took advantage of his slight lapse in concentration and snatched at the cabbage.

"Miss Doughbridge and . . . P.C. Keogh."

"Mr Keogh? What's he want?"

"Interfering with farmer's pigs," laughed Enid. "Perhaps they've found out you've got foot and mouth disease and are spreading it to animals."

"Come on," shouted Joyce. "It's not funny. They want you back now. You'll have to hurry."

Enid and Doreen stayed put as the Harris children ran off.

"I'm going home," said Doreen. "Pigs make your frock stink."

The four Harris children ran for all they were worth up Urchley Lane, towards Butt's Farm.

"What do you reckon it's all about, Joycie?" shouted a rather worried Wib.

''Search me.''

''Do you reckon it might be about the sheep nicking—or Old Stoopy perhaps?''

He stopped for a bit to catch his breath.

''Perhaps he wants me to go to court and give evidence, or present me with a medal—the Victoria Cross even for frightening them away.''

''They don't give Victoria Crosses to civilians, daft,'' countered Vee.

''But I'm not a civilian. I'm a school boy!''

They reached the gates of Butt's House and ran up the pathway to the front door. Standing in the hallway was Police Constable Keogh.

''In here please, lad,'' he said, in a very grave voice that didn't, in all honesty, indicate he was going to present Wib with a medal.

Standing in the dining room was Miss Doughbridge, and Miss Liggerty, as always, stood at her elbow. In the corner stood Mr Bixey, cap in hand. The children pushed into the room and P.C. Keogh closed the door behind them.

On Miss Doughbridge's highly-polished dining room table was a bicycle saddle-bag, which Wib had never seen before. Next to it was something he did however recognise. It was his cigarette tin, and in front of that in neat piles, laid out like evidence in a courtroom, were his picture cards. There was an awkward silence which made the tick of the clock over the mantelpiece sound even louder. Then Miss Doughbridge spoke.

"William, there is a very serious accusation against you . . . Mr Keogh, please."

She nodded permission for the policeman to speak.

"Er . . . seems, lad, that you've stolen one bike too many. We've caught you at it, red-handed, so to speak."

Wib was dumbfounded.

"Bikes? What bikes? I haven't pinched no bike. I haven't got a bike."

"He hasn't, mister," said Joyce.

"Be quiet, Joyce," snapped Miss Doughbridge. "Let him answer for himself. Mr Keogh?"

"I had a tip-off you were hiding a couple of bikes in the barn—we've had quite a few bikes stolen in the last few weeks—an 'epidemic' the papers have said—and, well, to cut a long story short, I examined your barn and found the bikes."

"I don't know what you're talking about. I never put them there, honest," protested Wib.

"Well then, how do you explain this tin and contents we found in this saddle-bag on one of the bikes?"

There was silence from Joyce, Vee and Freddy. They knew only too well who the Player's tin belonged to. But how could it have got in the saddle-bag?

"Well?" prompted Miss Doughbridge.

"You recognise the tin don't you, William?"

Wib bowed his head and said nothing. Miss Doughbridge persisted.

"It's yours, isn't it, William? It *is* yours."

Wib stared at the floor and nodded. Joyce once again spoke up for him.

"It's his tin all right, miss, but he wouldn't have taken the bikes—he doesn't even like bikes. We've been with him most of the time—we never saw him pinch anything—if you ask me someone's deliberately trying to get Wib into trouble."

"But we're not asking you, are we?" replied Miss Doughbridge.

P.C. Keogh coughed to get Miss Doughbridge's attention.

"Can I have a word with you *alone* please, miss."

The two of them stepped outside into the hall. The tick of the clock, like Wib's heartbeat, got so loud he thought it was going to explode.

Outside there was the sound of an engine turning over, and through the window Wib could see the policeman's car pulling out of the gates. At least he wouldn't be going to prison.

Miss Doughbridge returned and once more closed the doors behind her. Wib looked back at the carpet. He was completely innocent but there was no way this old battle-axe would ever believe him.

"Mr Keogh has taken a very kind and unnecessarily generous attitude about the whole affair. He's turning a blind eye to it all and has left the matter in my hands."

Joyce and Vee let out a sigh. But their relief was short-lived.

"Mr Bixey—the strap."

Mr Bixey stepped out from the corner and the children looked on in amazement as he began to unbuckle his thick leather belt.

"You're not going to hit him, Mr Bixey," shouted Joyce. "He's done nothing."

Miss Doughbridge turned towards Joyce and an evil, high-pitched scream came out of her red-painted mouth.

"You be quiet, young lady, and please do not speak until you are spoken to, Mr Bixey—the strap." Mr Bixey, his ruddy face drained of blood, spoke weakly to Miss Doughbridge.

"How many, miss?"

"Six."

Wilf Bixey's strong, knobbly hand took Wib by the collar and bent him over the high-backed dining chair. He pulled back the leather strap and, to Wib, it seemed forever before it made contact with his backside. But when it did, he knew it. He felt a yell in his throat but he managed to stifle it before it came out.

. . . Two . . . Three . . . Four . . . Mr Bixey held back as much as he could, but Miss Doughbridge's close attention ensured that he didn't cheat too much . . . Five . . . Six.

Mr Bixey put his belt back where it belonged, around his waist. Miss Liggerty, as always, had a famous saying ready for the occasion. She spoke out of the corner of her lop-sided mouth and popped her whelk-like eyes.

"Better it were that all the miseries which nature owns were ours at once than guilt."

"Quite so, Miss Liggerty," echoed Miss Doughbridge. "Very apt, very apt."

But Wib didn't think so. No saying in the world, however apt, could cool the burning he felt in the cheeks of his backside.

CHAPTER 16
WIBBLE WOBBLE

The canal by Cuffley Elbow had become Wib and Freddy's favourite place. It was very different from the canals they had left behind in Hackney. The Victorian navigators had cut it clearly and precisely through open fields, not through a busy crowded city. Consequently there were green banks and grassy verges instead of the backs of a thousand different factories.

True there were no low walls leading to treasure troves like the ball-bearing factory, where, if you crouched low enough to avoid the foreman, you would sneak away with pockets full of the shiny metal balls.

True there wasn't a hole in the fence that led to the furniture factory, where you could pick up odd-shaped pieces of wood—discarded chair legs that made beautiful make-believe tommy guns.

On the other hand, instead of murky water the colour of ox-tail soup, the canal here was almost clear, more blue than grey.

Then there were the locks. In London you could walk for miles before you even came to a lock. But in Wiltshire, where the land swept steeply up, the water level had to be raised drastically and there were locks every hundred yards or so, operated by long oak tillers that shifted huge metal cogs to open the sluice gates.

And best of all, unlike the canals of london, there were no "Cut Runners" to chase you along the tow-path. Those sour-faced individuals were employed specially to winkle out small boys like Wib and Freddy and stop them from getting up to mischief. They were generally elderly gentlemen, with no sense of humour and little understanding of the fascination of the waterways to young land-locked Londoners. If you allowed a Cut Runner to catch up with you, which was very rare, a sharp whack around the ankles with his stick would be your punishment.

At Cuffley Elbow, Freddy, Wib and Vee braved the cold wind and slight drizzle, waiting to see if they could catch sight of a water rat that had made its winter home in the canal bank under Lock Bridge. Freddy was more interested in his game of five-stones. He flicked them into the air with great skill.

Wib had been given an old pen-knife by Mr Bixey and he whittled away at a thick piece of wood.

"Suppose I made a big stake with a sharp point on it and hammered it through her heart, like Dracula."

"Don't be silly, Wib," said Vee, as she threw a twig into the water.

"On the other hand, I could tie her up and put her in Stubbs Tunnel and wait for a train to cut her in half."

"It wouldn't kill her," said Freddy. "She'd

probably still be alive—like a worm—then you'll have two Miss Doughbridge's wriggling away."

Vee tried to calm down her two moaning brothers.

"Stop complaining, you hardly ever see her and I'm not sure she's as bad as you say."

"You didn't get Old Bixey's belt, did you, clever boots!"

Wib's answer quietened her for a while, then Vee tried a different tack.

"It'll be Christmas in two weeks and Mum's coming."

"Who told you?"

"I think Mrs Bixey got a letter, but Joyce didn't want to tell you in case Mum changed her mind."

"Why should she change her mind?" asked Freddy.

"'Cos of Uncle Stanley. Ladies don't like leaving their fancy men, that's why." Wib answered in the superior voice he always put on for such worldly pronouncements.

"He's not her fancy man. He's going to be her new husband. Joycie told me!"

It was true that Joyce had told Vee. She'd also told her to cross her heart and not to dare tell Wib or Freddy.

"That means he'll be our dad," said Freddy.

"But we've already got a dad," Wib pointed out.

"Mum says in her letter that the police are trying to find him."

"Police?" said Wib. "Why the police? He's not done anything wrong, has he?"

"No. Course not. It's just that when people disappear the police have to look for 'em to tell them their missus don't want them anymore. Else it's bigga . . . bogga . . . something, anyway it's not allowed to have two husbands."

Wib used his sharp-pointed stick to fish out an old apple box that was floating down stream. In brown letters burned into the side, it said: "Jolly's Choice Cox's Apples. Wiltshire and London. Fresh daily."

"That's it! That's what we'll do!" screamed Wib.

"Do what?" said Freddy, who was now up to "crabsies" in his game of five-stones.

"We could build a raft. There's enough wood round here to build the *Queen Mary*."

"So?" asked Vee.

"So we can sail it down the canal—punt it even with a big stick. Perhaps find a horse to pull us. I've seen 'em do it with the barges—and take enough food . . ."

"Enough food?" inquired Vee. "How long do you expect to be away?"

"Forever, stupid. I'm talking about escaping for good!"

"Escape?" said Vee and Freddy, both

equally surprised at Wib's statement.

"This is a canal, isn't it? And we've got canals in Hackney—so it must join up somewhere."

"How do you know that?"

"'Cause the road over there is called 'The London Road', so this must be the London canal."

"But it might take *years*," said Freddy. "We might be old men with long grey beards before we got home."

"It's a stupid idea," said Vee, who was already disinterested and had started to walk back in the direction of Urchley Lane.

"No dafter than living here, clever boots!" Wib shouted after her, as she walked away. "We didn't want a bloody girl on the raft, anyway—three would probably sink it."

Freddy put his five-stones in his pocket and, to Wib's horror, also started back.

"Freddy, why don't you help me?"

"No."

"Why?"

"'Cause I'm going with Vee. I don't like water, anyway."

"Bloody traitors! I hope Old Drawbridge locks you in the cellar and gives you nothing to eat but horrible greens!"

Wib's words were lost on Freddy who had caught up with Vee. Wib became more and more angry, frantically collecting wood.

"I'll go on my own then. Sod the lot of you! I'm going back to Hackney where you don't get the blame for nicking things you haven't pinched."

Wib's double-dutch logic had very little effect on Freddy, who carried on walking. Wib kept on shouting.

"I'm leaving. You hear me?"

Freddy and Vee didn't even look around.

"We hear you."

"Where are you going?"

"We promised to meet Doreen and Arthur at Black Dog Farm. Bye."

Wib immediately dropped his sticks.

"Well, I might not be going today. I've got no string—but I'm going tomorrow. Mark my words." Obviously the sound of Black Dog Farm was just too inviting, and after a quick sprint, he caught up with the other two.

"You didn't get far," said Vee sarcastically.

"Shut your trap!"

Vee took the hint and said nothing for a minute or two.

"I know it's not nice being belted but there's no point in running away—you might drown," she said.

The three children walked through the field at the back of Frogshitch Farm and had reached as far as Urchley Lane before Wib replied.

"Drowning's not so bad. I don't even mind the belting. It's her steamed fish I can't stand."

Doreen and Arthur were waiting at the corner of Stoops Alley, outside the barber shop. Inside they could see Mr Spicer taking a steaming towel from a metal cabinet and placing it over a customer's face. As he patted it into place around the eyes, the man underneath let out a satisfied sigh.

Young Eric pulled out a plug in the round china basin and the dirty water gushed into a bucket below. Wib, Freddy and Arthur pressed their noses up against the window to watch the ritual of Eric lathering up the shaving brush. Mr Spicer caught sight of the inquisitive boys and shouted up the stairs for Cyril.

"Ciggywig, it's your mates for you."

Freddy and Wib giggled at Mr Spicer's nickname for his son. They would pull Cyril's leg about it later. Arthur remained silent. He was intrigued by the customer reclining in the barber's chair. Eric slowly removed the towel and began to lather the man's face. Arthur's eyes protruded from his head as he saw who the face belonged to.

"Look!" he whispered. "Look who it is having a shave!"

Wib and Freddy stopped giggling at "Ciggywig" just long enough to recognise the unmistakable features under the suds of the shaving soap. It was Old Stoopy.

The bell on the barber shop door made them all jump and they breathed a sigh of relief when they saw it was Cyril.

"What you looking at?"

"Ssh! It's Stoopy!"

Doreen and Vee had already got to the Mission Hall when the four boys ran past them.

"Quick, Vee, follow us."

"Why?"

"Just follow us!"

"Why are you running?"

"'Cause Stoopy's in the barber shop . . ."

"The barber shop?"

". . . and we want to have a look round the farm while he's away."

Doreen and Vee ran after the boys. Or more correctly, Vee ran; Doreen's actions could more accurately be described as wobbling. Arthur and Freddy chanted as she trailed behind them:

"My sister Kate,
She's a soppy date,
Wibble, wobble, wibble, wobble,
Jelly on the plate."

Whoever Kate was in the old rhyme, she obviously ran just like Doreen Noblock.

The children climbed over the wall by the "Private—No Admittance" sign that Old Stoopy had erected. Even if they'd seen it, they probably wouldn't have taken any notice. The farm was still in a sorry state of repair—much the same as when Old Critchley had left it—but there was a dead feeling about the place that made it very different to all the other farms around Pottley. Even the birds didn't seem to like it there. Arthur remarked that he felt more at home in St Mary's graveyard.

Pulling themselves up on the low window-sill they peeped into the kitchen of the old house. Stoopy was obviously living there, but he would have won no prizes for house-keeping; the inside of the house closely resembled the pig-sty at Frogshitch Farm.

Across the yard was a big wooden barn. Hanging from the steel tie-bar was the only visible new addition to the farm; a large metal lock.

"Wonder what's in there?" Wib whispered.

"Search me," Doreen whispered back.

"Why is everyone whispering," said Freddy in a loud voice.

"Ssh . . . 'cause we shouldn't be here."

"But Stoopy's miles away."

"Yeah, but you don't know who else might be here, do you?" Wib snapped back at his brother.

"Who?" He spoke in a whisper this time.

"Someone you haven't even thought of could just be hanging about. It all depends . . ."

"Depends on what?" asked Arthur.

"What's he talking about?" Freddy scratched his head and turned to Cyril, who was equally dumbfounded by Wib's somewhat confusing, melodramatic whispering.

"Search me."

"Look," said Vee. "There's a door up there where they hoist up the hay and stuff."

"Right," said Wib, taking control. "Cyril, Arthur, get that rope from around the tarpaulin over that tractor and we'll throw it over the pulley, then you can tie it around me and pull me up."

"Why you?" Doreen asked indignantly.

"'Cause I'm the best climber. That's why."

"You're not!" Vee disputed. "I am."

Wib was stumped for a moment. She was undoubtedly more agile than he was.

"Ah, but I thought of it first, didn't I?"

Vee was still not convinced, but reluctantly agreed to let Wib go up on the rope. After three attempts, Cyril managed to loop the rope over the pulley wheel. It was then firmly secured around Wib's waist by two 'sailor's knots', expertly applied by Arthur who said his uncle was once in the navy. Vee, Doreen, Cyril and Freddy pulled together on the rope and hoisted Wib slowly upwards, until he was level with the metal bar that held the pulley wheel. With one hand on the rope and one on the bar, he managed to heave himself into the hole at the top of the barn.

"What can you see?" shouted Freddy, as loudly as he dare. Wib's answer shocked them all.

"Dead bodies!"

"Stop joking," said Vee, not quite sure if he was or not.

"I'm not joking. There's blood everywhere. It's horrible."

The four children standing below were horrified. Cyril's normally fat rosy cheeks went white.

"Let's go," he said, "before we get caught."

Freddy shouted up at Wib once more.

"You *are* joking, Wib. Seriously, are you joking?"

"I'm not joking! God's honour. There's hundred's of 'em hanging by hooks—some of them have had their legs chopped off!"

They could see by his face he was telling the truth. Vee and Doreen started to panic, which scared poor windy Cyril so much he was already half way to the gate.

"Listen. I've got to go now, you lot. I've just remembered my tea will be on the table. See you."

"Make sure Stoopy don't catch you on your own!" Arthur's warning stopped Cyril in his tracks.

"All right, I'll wait for you. But don't play silly buggers—hurry up and let's go."

Arthur had an inquisitive smile on his little mole-like face. He'd read all about mass murderers in his dad's *Sunday Graphic*, and was quite excited by Wib's discovery.

''Who are all the people,'' he asked.

''What people?'' answered Wib, rather surprised at the question.

''The dead bodies.''

''They're not people, you daft 'appath. They're sheep! Dead sheep's carcasses!''

CHAPTER 17
MUM

Mrs Bixey knocked on Joyce and Vee's door and cheerfully called out her usual morning greeting.

"Tea's up. Wake up. No more snoring, it's morning."

Vee propped herself up in the bed and rubbed her eyes. Outside she could see a coating of white frost on the windows, which made Mrs Bixey's hot tea even more welcome than usual.

"Is it snow?"

"No, love, but it's a frosty one. It wouldn't surprise me if we got some snow. Sky's right for it."

"No chance," said Joyce. "It never snows at Christmas—except on the Christmas cards. It was foggy last year in Hackeny—couldn't see a hand in front of you."

Joyce stretched out her arms to yawn, but quickly snatched them back under the bed clothes when she realised how chilly it was.

"What time is it?"

"Half past seven and shake a leg." Mrs Bixey poured a kettle of hot water into the china bowl on the sideboard. "You've got a lot of smartening up to do if you're going to look decent for your mother.''

Vee had almost forgotten. It was Saturday already and Mrs Harris had written to say that she and Siddy were coming to see them.

''Do you reckon she'll really come?'' said Vee, pouring her tea into the saucer to cool it—much to the disapproval of Mrs Bixey.

''That's enough of them London habits, Vee. You mind you watch your manners, else you'll grow up with a curly tail.''

Downstairs Mr Bixey was busy cleaning his boots on the kitchen table. It wasn't just for Mrs Harris' benefit, either. It was his normal Saturday morning ritual. He'd lay out an old newspaper, pour out his tea, light up a pipe and brush away for half an hour, stopping at regular intervals for a puff, a sip and a spit.

''Cup more tea please, Fay,'' he shouted out.

''What did your last servant die of, Wilf Bixey?'' came back the reply. ''Get it yourself!''

''I'm doing my boots.''

In the corner of the kitchen was a large Christmas tree. It wasn't really a Christmas tree but something similar that Joyce had found growing down by Oven Bottom. Not that the Harris children would have known the difference, because it was the first one they'd ever had.

Vee and Joyce had made all sorts of decorations out of milk bottle tops, which looked almost as good as the real thing. Mrs Bixey had cut out a cardboard fairy and covered it in silver paper.

Across the yard, at Butt's House, Wib and Freddy had already been up for half an hour. Miss Liggerty had woken them at seven, and two plates of luke warm porridge later they were ready for a walk in Urchley Lane. Freddy poked his head out of the front door. There was a thin covering of freezing frost everywhere. Even the water pump had an icicle hanging from its nozzle.

"It's a bit nippy out here, Wib! The water pump's frozen."

"What time have we got to meet Mum?" said Wib, from inside the slightly warmer hall.

"Not till eleven. There's bags of time."

"Right. I'll race you down to Sir Percy's statue." The two brothers tore off down the lane, skilfully skirting around the frozen-over puddles, almost as if they weren't there.

At Devizes, the narrow railway platform was crowded with evacuee families waiting for the London train. The chilling December wind cut through the station, leaving red noses and stinging ears.

"Shift your backside, dearie, thank you. Morning."

There was no mistaking the loud rasping voice of the lady with the carbuncles. She was wearing a black coat with an astrakhan collar that was far too smart to have been her own.

Unfortunately, she had slightly spoiled her otherwise elegant appearance by wearing a green turban and Wellington boots.

Mr Bixey tried to avoid her by pretending his bootlace was undone, but she had already spotted him.

"Wotcha, cock, remember me?"

"Oh, ah. Morning, ma'am." Bixey raised his cap, more out of habit than politeness.

"They've got a bloody nerve—you seen this?" she rasped.

Mr Bixey was taken by the arm and dragged off with a familiarity not really representative of their two brief meetings. At the back of the platform she pointed at a Government poster that had been recently put up. Beneath a gold emblem of the crown, it proclaimed:

"*Your* courage
Your cheerfulness
Your resolution
WILL BRING US VICTORY."

Mr Bixey read it and took off his hat to scratch his head, the way he always did when he was lost for an answer.

"Oh, ah, quite right. That's the spirit," he offered.

"Quite bloody right? You must be joking, mate. *Your* courage. *Your* cheerfulness. That's me and you, mate. Will bring *us* victory—that's *them*, mate. Bloody cheek. I'm going to find the geezer who put this up and tell him where he should have stuck it!''

She stormed off down the platform in the direction of the station master's office. Bixey scratched his head once more and re-read the poster to fathom out the reason for her anger.

Along the platform Wib and Freddy were giggling uncontrollably at an advertisement for Madame Maureen's shop ''Underwear de Paris''. There was a drawing of a young lady with very little on and underneath it said: ''French Knickers, Cami-Knickers. Satin and crepe.'' Seeing the word ''Knickers'' standing out in red printer's type amused Wib and Freddy in a way which Vee and Joyce failed to understand.

There was a loud cheer from the rest of the platform crowd and a great surge forward as the London train steamed round the hillside and pulled to a halt in the station.

The doors rattled open and out jumped soldiers, relatives, sweethearts, and most important of all, Mrs Harris and Siddy.

''Mum! Siddy!'' The four children left Mr Bixey far behind as they weaved their way through the kissing couples and re-united families.

Mrs Harris looked very smart in a new winter coat and hat. She pretended not to cry as she hugged and kissed the children. Joyce also made a bad job at hiding her tears; in order not to look too soppy, she picked up Siddy and threw him in the air. Vee, Wib and Freddy bombarded Vi Harris with more questions than she could answer.

''Have we got a new house, yet?''

''Are there still bombs in London?''

''How's Darkie, did you see him?''

''How long are you staying for?''

''No chance of some chocolate, is there?''

''Where's your case?''

The last question was the only one to get an answer, and it wasn't the one they had expected.

''Uncle Stanley's got it.''

Mrs Harris stopped hugging Vee for a moment and nodded towards Stanley, who was respectfully standing about five yards away.

''Stan, come and say hello. Kids, this is Uncle Stanley.''

''Hello.'' The four children politely smiled at him.

''He's older than our other dad,'' Freddy whispered to Wib.

Uncle Stanley was about forty years old, tall with Brylcreemed hair and a square jaw that jutted out like a fighter pilot's. He could possibly have been described as handsome but for his bad teeth that closely resembled a piano keyboard.

''Don't suppose you brought any chocolate with you, did you, Uncle?''

Wib said the word ''uncle'' without conviction.

''Now don't get greedy, you wait and see,''

said Mrs Harris. "Let's be getting on."

She and Uncle Stanley walked along the platform and shook hands with Mr Bixey. As always, he politely raised his cap, murmured an "Oh, ah" to Mrs Harris, and shook Uncle Stanley firmly by the hand.

The bus ride to Pottley was probably the noisiest the Wiltshire Bus Company had ever experienced. Mrs Harris sat patiently through a dozen wonderful stories about the countryside from Wib, Vee and Freddy. Joyce ran through the list of films she had seen and described to Uncle Stanley in detail her favourite scenes.

There was however no mention of Black Dog Farm or the belting. Old Stoopy was a secret that only belonged to the children, Doreen, Cyril and Arthur. As for the belting—Wib had made everyone promise not to tell Mum. He only hoped Miss Doughbridge didn't mention it.

The children laughed as Mrs Harris awkwardly tried to manoeuvre the puddles in Urchley Lane. She managed to get away with nothing more than a soggy left foot. Uncle Stanley was less fortunate. With great show and bravado he attempted to leap over the puddle, but had the bad luck to land on a piece of ice which sent his legs in two different directions, leaving him on his backside in the water. Mr Bixey joined in the laughter as he offered a strong arm to help him out.

Mrs Bixey and Mrs Harris got on very well

together and, much to the childrens' delight, so did Mr Bixey and Uncle Stanley. Admittedly the two men were helped by a few pints of Mr Bixey's brown ale and a bottle of whisky Stanley had conjured up from his bottomless mackintosh pocket. The same miraculous pocket also provided a bag of half-hour gobstoppers, five Mars bars, and half a pound of Rowntree's Milk and Plain. Mrs Bixey had hung up Stanley's trousers to dry over the black kitchen range and he kept everyone in fits of laughter doing a sand dance in his long-john underpants.

Suddenly the children stopped laughing as they heard the bell ring above the fireplace. Uncle Stanley wondered why he'd lost his audience so abruptly.

"What's up? Who's that, Father Christmas?"

"It means Miss Doughbridge wants Mr Bixey," Joyce explained.

"Oh, ah," said Bixey, quickly putting on his coat and hat and rubbing his shoes on the backs of his trouser legs. "Best not to keep her waiting. I'll be right back—help yourself to another pint of brown ale."

Bixey quickly slipped out of the door.

"What's she like, the old girl?" said Mrs Harris.

"All right," said Wib, without hesitation.

"Look after you all right, does she?"

"Food's not much cop, the boiled fish is

diabolical and the porridge is lumpy . . .''

''And there's not a fish and chip shop in the whole place,'' added Freddy, trying to change the subject from Miss Doughbridge.

''. . . but otherwise it's all right . . .'' Wib noticed that Mrs Bixey had returned from the kitchen. ''. . . and wait till you've had Mrs Bixey's spotted dick.''

''And her homemade mince pies,'' Vee joined in. ''And we get egg and bacon every morning.''

''Goodness me, you wouldn't credit there was a war on, would you?'' said Mrs Harris. ''Not like London.''

Mr Bixey returned from Butt's House with the message that Miss Doughbridge would see Mrs Harris straight away. Politely he explained that Uncle Stanley wasn't invited.

''I'd best take you over now, love.''

Five minutes with Miss Doughbridge had sobered him up somewhat and the children saw that his beery smile had left his face.

Mrs Harris walked across the yard towards Butt's House and noticed that it had started to snow. Mr Bixey made a swift exit and left her standing alone in the hall. Miss Doughbridge came out of her bedroom door, preceded by her two cats, fat Cane and the skinny, nervous Abel. The old woman spoke from the shadows at the top of the stairs—almost as if Mrs Harris had a contagious disease which she might catch. She called out in her haughty, high-pitched voice, which frightened Mrs Harris no less than it did the children.

"How long are you staying?"

"Just the three days."

"It's not possible for you to stay here, at this house."

"It's all right, love, Mr Bixey's kindly fixed me, Siddy and . . . er . . . my fiancé up with a room at the Bell Inn."

Miss Doughbridge didn't like being called "love", any more than Stanley would have liked being called a "fiancé".

Out of the corner of her eye Mrs Harris could see Miss Liggerty, who was peeping through a crack in the kitchen door. Miss Doughbridge continued the strained conversation.

"They're very undisciplined children."

"A bit high-spirited that's all, but they've got good natures," replied Mrs Harris, a little scared at arguing with the voice at the top of the stairs.

"They're in need of discipline, and I'm not a well woman. I wish you could impress this upon them. This is not a hotel. This is our home and they should respect that. We don't want your money. Please take the postal orders you sent. They're on the hallstand to your right."

Mrs Harris looked at the envelope she had sent with the weekly six shillings a child contribution that the Government had asked evacuee parents to pay.

"Oh, I do wish you'd take the money. I can afford it now . . ."

"We don't want to be beholden to you. What we do is because we're good Christians, not because of monetary gain."

"As you like," said Mrs Harris. "I'll have a word with them to make sure they behave. I hope they're not too much trouble for you."

"They are," said Miss Doughbridge, turning to go to her room, "but Jesus has asked us and we have obeyed. Goodbye, Mrs Harris. Please make sure the door is closed behind you."

"Bye, miss . . . er . . . Merry Christmas . . ." But the only reply Mrs Harris got from the lady of Butt's House was the closing of her bedroom door. At the end of the hall Miss Liggerty was still watching.

"Merry Christmas to you, too."

"Merry Christmas," came back the whining reply.

"Looks like a white one, after all," said Mrs Harris. But there was no hope of any more conversation with Miss Liggerty, because she too had closed her door.

Under the aloof stares of Cane and Abel, Mrs Harris picked up her postal orders and hurried out the door. In the yard, the snow had begun to settle. But, somehow, it wasn't nearly as cold as in Miss Doughbridge's hall.

CHAPTER 18
THE WANDERING JUNK MAN

Christmas morning Joyce pulled back the curtains and saw the kind of view she thought only existed on Christmas cards. Overnight the countryside had turned from a lush green to pure white. Across Butt's Field, through the crisp, clean air, she could see the snow-clad roof tops of Pottley village.

Wib and Freddy had also seen the snow and for once were up before Miss Liggerty banged on the door to waken them.

"Awake already, miss," shouted Wib. In fact they had been up for hours and had sneaked out by way of their secret staircase to touch the newly-fallen snow. Wib had grabbed Freddy by the arm as he rushed out of the tiny concealed door.

"Don't!"

"Why not?" asked Freddy, annoyed at the tight grip his brother had on his jersey.

"'Cause they'll see our footprints, stupid—in the snow—then they'll find out about the staircase."

Instead the two boys neatly scraped off an inch of snow from the surface and touched it to their lips. It tasted almost as delicious as Granny Elliott's penny drinks, back in Hackney.

Miss Doughbridge's bell rang at Butt's Farm

and Mr Bixey hurried across the yard. Before he was half way up the path Miss Liggerty opened the door and called out.

"Bring the two girls, Mr Bixey."

"I think they're still eating their breakfast, miss."

"Right away, Mr Bixey. Miss Doughbridge would like to see them."

"Certainly, miss. Right away."

Miss Liggerty asked Wib, Freddy, Joyce and Vee to wait in the hall.

"Miss Doughbridge will see you in a minute. No noise or playing around. And, William, please don't play with the hats."

Wib had been told off more than once for trying on the comical ladies' hats hanging on the hallstand.

Whatever it was Miss Doughbridge wanted it was obviously a special occasion, because they had never been allowed into her "best parlour" before. Miss Liggerty emerged from the room.

"Come in, please."

Inside, surrounded by unlived-in furniture, sat Miss Doughbridge, in a chintzy, high-backed chair. Dozing in her lap was fat Cane, who purred contentedly as his owner stroked his back with her white bony hand. The room had the unmistakable Butt's House smell of Mansion Polish and cats, but in the fireplace was a very rare and unusual sight; a roaring fire. And on the table by the window, sitting in the middle of the maroon chenille cloth, was an even stranger sight. If Wib didn't know better, it looked remarkably like wrapped-up Christmas presents. Also, there was a black lacquered tray with a bottle of sherry and a number of small crystal glasses. Wib knew there was no chance of a drink, but the sight of the presents made him cross his fingers behind his back.

Miss Doughbridge spoke as friendly as her shrill, starchy voice would allow.

"Merry Christmas, children."

"Merry Christmas, Miss Doughbridge."

"I suppose you're off to see your parents . . . er . . . your mother and the gentleman."

"Yes, miss, then we're going into Devizes for a Christmas show that the Evacuees Reception Committee are putting on."

Joyce spoke hurriedly but politely; it seemed that Christmas had finally softened even Miss Doughbridge's tough old hide. Vee also sensed the change in attitude.

"Then we're going for a sing-song at the Mission Hall—the Sally Army are running a talent contest, and Wib's going to do his Tommy Handley jokes and I'm going to sing."

"A carol, I trust," chipped in Miss Liggerty.

"No, miss, 'White Cliffs of Dover'."

"Don't worry, miss," said Wib wryly, "her voice is so rotten it'll probably sound like 'Good King Wenseslas'."

"New cardigans, I see."

''Yes, miss,'' answered Vee, ''Mrs Bixey knitted them. We helped her unwind the wool from one of Mr Bixey's woollies—there was enough for both of us.''

''Very nice, too. Well, as it's Christmas, Miss Liggerty and I would like you to have some gifts we have bought you.''

''Thank you very much, miss, that's very kind,'' said Vee, who was a little too gushing for Wib's liking. Christmas or no Christmas, he still hated the lady with no face.

''But before you open them, I think it only right and proper we get into the Christmas spirit by singing a few carols. Miss Liggerty, could you hand out the hymnals, please?''

The children took one book each and watched while Miss Liggerty took a key from the blue china pot and opened the top of a polished desk, revealing the yellowed keys of the old pump organ. They smiled as Miss Liggerty vigorously pounded the foot pedals before the strangled notes emerged from the organ tubes. They quickly raced through ''Come All Ye Faithful'', ''There Were Three Kings'', and capped it off with ''Once In Royal David's City''.

Miss Doughbridge's high-pitched voice seemed to be singing a different set of notes to most mortals, and certainly different to the ones Miss Liggerty was bashing out on the organ.

''Miss Liggerty . . . the presents.''

Miss Doughbridge's faithful companion

wiped her mouth with her handkerchief. She was quite out of breath from the pumping and looked more like she'd been running around Hawk's Field than playing a musical instrument.

"Can we open them now, miss?"

"You can, but don't tear the paper too much. It's very hard to come by and should be used again."

The children carefully undid their presents. Each parcel revealed a book—secondhand by the look of them. Joyce's was *The Pilgrim's Progress* by John Bunyan, which in all honesty didn't look too inviting—a sort of religious book. She flicked through the pages and was a bit put off by the austere colour pictures of a man in armour. Vee it seemed was a bit luckier. She had *Gulliver's Travels* which she had heard serialised on the radio. Miss Liggerty had written in the front "Remember Vee, in Lilliput Gulliver was a giant, but in Brobdingnag he was but a dwarf."

The quotation was lost on Vee, but at least the book looked a bit more interesting than Joyce's. Freddy and Wib had two different volumes of *The Childrens' Almanac*. Wib would have preferred *Biggles Defies The Swastika*, but changed his mind when he saw there was a whole chapter on collecting picture cards.

The children thanked the two elderly ladies and backed out of the parlour door, wishing them Merry Christmas. For a brief moment, as the logs crackled on the fire, the Misses Doughbridge and Liggerty looked almost human.

The snow at Oven Bottom was almost a foot deep and Freddy and Wib ploughed through it, rolling over and over like human snowballs. In Cheddar Gorge, the snow had drifted against the bank and was five feet thick in places, with the result that Vee completely disappeared after one ambitious leap-frog.

The coffins in the undertaker's garden were also filled with snow and looked like giant versions of the flour scoops in Noblock's grocery shop.

The high street was also crisp and white. In Hackney by now the busy traffic would have churned the pure white snow into a nasty grey slush. In Pottley however, apart from the deep grooves caused by Mr Bootwick's breakdown lorry, the snow was undisturbed. The water trough had completely frozen over; the ice was so thick Wib couldn't even break it with the cast-iron drinking cup, which he swung on the end of its chain.

At the Bell Inn, they were allowed upstairs to where Mrs Harris was staying with Siddy and Uncle Stanley. Siddy had already opened his presents and greeted them with a 'whizzer' on the end of a piece of string. He vigorously swung it round, accidentally catching Freddy under the chin. Siddy caught a whack across the head for his clumsiness.

Mrs Harris' presents for the children looked

rather pathetic, wrapped up as they were in an assortment of brown paper and old newspapers. Such was the shortage of coloured Christmas paper in London. But it was what was inside that mattered. For Joyce it was a necklace and a bakelite compact with real face-powder. Vee had a jig-saw of King George's coronation and a game of Happy Families. Freddy unwrapped a clockwork tank and a re-painted Dinky toy of a post office van. Wib unravelled an old copy of the *Daily Mirror* to reveal a new set of film star picture cards.

"What about Mum's present?" he said, in the middle of scrutinizing the back of Clark Gable.

"Oh, sorry, nearly forgot." Joyce gave her mother a small neatly-wrapped parcel. Mrs Harris opened it with almost as much excitement as the children.

"What is it?" she said, a little puzzled.

"It's a kettle-holder," said Vee. "Mrs Bixey helped us knit it."

"You put it round the kettle to stop you burning your hand," Freddy explained.

"Very nice," said Mrs Harris.

"We're sorry we didn't buy you anything, Uncle Stanley," said Wib.

"That's all right, son."

"Only we didn't know you was going to be our new dad, you see. We just thought you were her fancy man."

Naturally enough there was a rather awkward

silence as Wib's remark dropped like a punctured barrage balloon. Joyce nervously opened and closed her compact and pretended not to have heard. Mrs Harris was the most embarrassed of all and twiddled her new kettle holder. Uncle Stanley smiled and eased the situation by changing the subject.

"Right then, you lot, who's coming to this concert?"

"We are!" There was a noisy commotion as the children put on their coats and scrambled down the narrow staircase. Uncle Stanley stroked Mrs Harris' hair and gave her a kiss on the forehead. She stopped twiddling the kettle holder.

"Sorry, Stan. They didn't mean no harm."

The concert at the Palace was organised by Mrs Knapp-Jenkins, who took it in turns with Mr Fishpool, the town clerk, to introduce the different acts. The 'professionals' were on first.

"Now, children and parents . . . and others . . ." boomed Mr Fishpool. He stuttered a bit and had no right to be master of ceremonies; but as Mrs Harris pointed out, he had a lot of pluck. With a name like Fishpool, he needed it.

"Mr Spellgrove, our conjuror from Wooton Bassett, will leave you spellbound . . ."

He laughed at his play on words, and so did the enthusiastic audience. Mr Spellgrove turned out to be an awful magician and Wib saw through all his tricks, but it was Christmas and so everyone "ooed" and "aahed" with amazement at his every move.

Miss Audrey Fishpool, the town clerk's daughter, gave a recital from *The Desert Song*, singing "One Alone" and accompanying herself on the piano accordian, which she squeezed with great gusto.

A novelty act was next, featuring a local man from Wadsworth Breweries who rattled his set of false teeth to the tune of "Let Him Go, Let Him Tarry". This made Wib and Freddy laugh so much they had to go to the lavatory to relieve themselves.

Then came an unexpected treat. Mr Austin, the cinema manager, went up on stage and lifted his hands to hush the excited crowd, who by now were ready to applaud anybody—even balding cinema managers.

"Ladies, gentlemen, children—we are indeed in luck today. Calling in to this cinema, as he did, just by chance enables the management of the Palace to proudly present to you . . . star of theatre and radio—the Wandering Junk Man. Yes, it's your very own Syd Walker . . ."

There was a cheer from the audience that must have caused the roof timbers permanent damage. In came radio's "Wandering Junk Man"; he was instantly beseiged by everyone asking for autographs. Hundreds of hands held out scraps of paper, evacuation leaflets, gas-mask boxes—anything that could take his signature.

For a good half an hour there was total pandemonium and only when Mr Fishpool and Mr Austin pulled him towards the exit, did things get back to normal. There was excited chatter as people sat back in their seats. To think, they'd actually seen and even touched Syd Walker. The funny thing was, a good ninety per cent of them had never heard of him.

The talent contest was introduced by Mrs Knapp-Jenkins, who thanked Mrs Westmead who was kindly going to play the piano.

Altogether there were ten different versions of ''White Cliffs of Dover'' and Vee's wasn't nearly the worst by a long chalk. Wib's Tommy Handley jokes were well received by the audience, but he went and spoiled it by getting over confident and forgetting the words of ''Umbrella Man''.

The little blond-haired girl on the evacuee train sang ''Good Ship Lollypop'' once more; half way through she clutched herself and ran off crying.

''Mum, I've done it again! I want to go to the lav!''

This brought the house down and the girl was immediately announced the winner by Mr Fishpool; but unfortunately the girl's mother couldn't persuade her to come out of the ladies' toilet to collect her prize.

On the way back to Butt's House they bumped into Mr Bixey, who was returning from the George & Dragon. After a few tots from

Uncle Stanley's hip flask the two men stripped off their jackets and embarked on a game of British Bulldog, which resulted in them both falling on their backsides in the snow. Then Uncle Stanley suggested a hopping race to Frogshitch Farm. They skidded and tripped all over the place on the slippery surface. Mr Bixey, puffing heavily, gave up half way when he saw the stern figure of Miss Liggerty standing at the gate.

"Morning, miss," said Bixey, raising an imaginary hat, embarrassed to be caught with his jacket off.

"Afternoon, Bixey. Miss Doughbridge wondered if you and Mrs Harris and her . . . friend, would like to partake in a glass of sherry. Although by the look of you, I dare say you've had sufficient."

"Certainly, miss. We'd be honoured. Most certainly."

Miss Liggerty went back up the path. Mrs Harris and Uncle Stanley embraced one another and started laughing. Wib was still very doubtful.

"Mind the old cow don't poison you!"

Christmas lunch at the Bixey's was a feast the Harris children would remember for the rest of their lives. Mr Bixey, still a little drunk from the brown ale, sherry and Uncle Stanley's whisky, proceeded to carve delicious white slices off the biggest turkey they had ever seen.

Afterwards there were mince pies and Christmas pudding, which they managed to squeeze down into their already full stomachs. How Mrs Bixey got over the war-time rationing and shortages that everyone in London was suffering was a total mystery to Mrs Harris. Mrs Bixey said she had an "arrangement" at Noblock's the grocers which allowed for such things—for the time being, anyway.

Uncle Stanley and Mr Bixey slept off their whisky and brown ale, snoring loudly, slumped in the two armchairs in front of the fire. The two women finished the washing up and took the children to the carol singing at the Mission Hall.

The evening was filled with an impromptu concert in which everyone joined in. Wib sang "Umbrella Man"—properly this time—and Uncle Stanley belted out some rude songs that made the children laugh but Mrs Harris blush. Even Freddy did his impersonation of Arthur Askey, the radio comedian, singing "Busy, Busy Bee". Joyce did the waltz with Uncle Stanley. Mr Bixey did his version of the fox-trot with Mrs Harris—leaving her with feet a little flatter than when she began. There was Tizer for everyone and Uncle Stanley appeared to have an inexhaustible supply of Mars bars. When you'd gone without for so long, each one seemed like a bar of gold. There were also plates of Mrs Bixey's honeycomb, which she had miraculously made from golden syrup and bicarbonate.

The evening seemed to go on for hours, and

the noisier they got the more Joyce expected Miss Doughbridge to ring the bell from across the yard; but she didn't. Obviously she was sleeping off the effects of her unaccustomed glass of sherry.

It was then that the long evening came to a sudden and cruel end. And, for once, Miss Doughbridge had nothing to do with it. Uncle Stanley pulled Mrs Bixey out of her easy chair to join in the Hokey-Cokey with the rest of them.

"Come on, Fay, don't want no wall-flowers at this party."

Mrs Bixey roared with laughter, almost spilling her glass of port and lemon as she stood up. Suddenly, she clutched her chest with her fat podgy hands and collapsed unconscious on to the ground, knocking over the Christmas tree as she fell. Uncle Stanley picked her up and lay her in a chair, while Mr Bixey slapped her face to bring her round. The children just watched.

"It's her ticker," he blurted out. "It's her heart."

No one had ever mentioned a weak heart to the children—there was no reason at all why they should. They had never seen anyone die before. It just couldn't be possible. Not so quickly. Only moments ago she was singing loudly, and now . . . she was gone. It seemed like a horrible nightmare but it was all painfully true. The children stood and watched in silence as Mr Bixey sobbed his heart out into his dead wife's lap.

In a matter of seconds, the best Christmas

they could have dreamed of had turned into the worst Christmas they had ever known.

CHAPTER 19
RED-HANDED

Mrs Harris stayed on for Mrs Bixey's funeral, but Uncle Stanley had to get back to London. Mrs Harris was a little frightened of Miss Doughbridge without Stanley around to back her up, and when she returned from the funeral she was summoned across to Butt's House.

Miss Liggerty showed her into the dining room and put a cup of tea on the table in front of her. Miss Doughbridge walked in the door, dragging her bad leg behind her.

"Good morning, Mrs Harris."

"Morning, miss." Miss Doughbridge eased herself onto one of the high-backed dining chairs and rested her thin hands on the handle of her walking stick. Miss Liggerty stood at her elbow and the ever present Cane and Abel lay at her feet.

"Tragic events. Very tragic. Mrs Bixey was a good woman. A very good woman."

"I know. Everyone's very upset. I feel very sorry for Mr Bixey. He's beside himself. He don't know whether he's coming or going."

"It is very clear that your children cannot remain at Butt's Farm."

"No."

"Mr Bixey cannot possibly cope with looking

after them on his own."

"No. I understand that." Mrs Harris shifted uncomfortably in her seat and nervously fidgeted with her hair. Miss Doughbridge's small grey-blue eyes were bright and piercing in the middle of her powdered, featureless face.

"Er . . . I thought I'd pop into Devizes and have a word with Mrs . . . er . . . Knapp . . . what's-her-name—the billeting lady. So's the girls can perhaps move somewhere else."

"That won't be necessary," answered Miss Doughbridge coldly. "They will stay here. Miss Liggerty can look after four as well as two. There is ample room. And Miss Liggerty would welcome the challenge."

"Oh, no, I wouldn't want to trouble you . . ."

Miss Doughbridge wasn't listening; she waved her bony hand as Miss Liggerty helped her out of her chair.

"It's settled then. I suggest they move their things over here immediately. Miss Liggerty has already prepared their beds."

The four children shifted across to Butt's House in complete silence. At the door of the farm, Joyce looked back down the hallway that was once warm and cosy. Mrs Bixey had gone forever and the wonderful smell of homemade bread had vanished from the kitchen.

At the end of Urchley Lane the children

waited quietly until the single-decker bus arrived from Pewsey. The snow had already started to melt as Mrs Harris kissed them goodbye. Joyce as usual was the most upset.

"Don't worry, love, it's very unfortunate about Mrs Bixey—she was a nice old lady, but we all have to die sometime."

"It's not that, it's . . ."

"It's what?"

"It's . . ."

Wib finished the sentence for her.

"It's Old Drawbridge. We can't stand her and the girls don't want to stay with her. Neither do Freddy and me. The porridge is lumpy and the beds are damp."

"Come on, missus," said the lady bus conductor. "Haven't got all day. You've had all Christmas to say hello and goodbye."

"Who's house do you want to stay in?"

"Cyril's."

"Arthur's."

"Doreen's."

The three younger children each came back with their own selfish solution, which angered Mrs Harris. She shook her head and lifted Siddy onto the bus.

"Now you listen to me, you lot. Life ain't all it's cracked up to be now and again. It's not all cowboys and indians and free flicks. There *is* a war on and we've all got to put up with a lot of things we don't bloody like. I've had to—now you'll have to. So stop snivelling and buckle under."

"Finished, missus?" said the rather disagreeable bus conductress. "Or are we going to be waiting here all day?"

Mrs Harris picked up her hold-all and climbed onto the platform as the bus moved off.

She and Siddy waved out of the rear window, but the four children walked off down Urchley Lane without looking back. In a way they felt let down. At the bottom of the lane the snow had melted, and the puddles seemed bigger than ever.

During the next few weeks, Arthur, Cyril, Doreen, Vee, Freddy and Wib took it in turns to keep watch on Old Stoopy at Black Dog Farm. They would lie on top of the hill at Dingle's Piece, looking through Arthur's new binoculars and noting down all the comings and goings in a "daily log". Arthur had said this would be necessary for court evidence.

They had already recorded the regular visits of two butchers from Devizes; Mr Wilson, the manager of Perrymead's Animal Food Purveyors, was another frequent visitor.

Wib, Freddy and Arthur lay on an old army groundsheet in the long grass, taking turns to look through the binoculars. The ground underneath them was hard with frost and Wib stood up to rub his sore knees. Suddenly he saw a new visitor to Stoopy's farm; it was the truck from

Bootwick's Motor Repairs.

"Look you two, it's Frog Eyes' dad's lorry!"

Sure enough, Mr Bootwick climbed out of the cab and, to Wib's amazement and glee, so did Frog Eyes himself; young Master Gilbert Bootwick.

The three boys watched with open mouths as the back of the truck was unloaded and Mr Bootwick took down six sparkling new Hudson bicycles—exactly like the ones P.C. Keogh had found at Butt's Farm. Stoopy wheeled the bikes into the barn, and out came Mr Bootwick with two sheep's carcasses over his shoulder. He took out a quart of Wadsworth Brown Ale from the cab and walked across to the house. Young Gilbert was excluded from such wheeling and dealing and sat on the running-board, reading a copy of *Hotspur*.

"Right," said Wib. "We've caught 'em red-handed. You two run and get old Keogh. But hurry up. We haven't got long."

"We've got about as long as a bottle of brown ale," added Arthur wisely.

"How about you?" Freddy asked Wib. "What are you going to do? Why aren't you going? Why is it always us?"

"I'm going to stop here and watch what they do—what they get up to. Get going! Quick! And Arthur, leave the binoculars."

Wib watched as Freddy and Arthur hared down the hill at Dingle's Piece, across the fields in the direction of the Mission Hall and Sloops Alley. The Pottley police station was a tiny converted shop next door to Belcher's Hardware, and Wib crossed his fingers that they'd find P.C. Keogh at home. For some reason he remembered his mother's old saying that there was always plenty of coppers around—except when you needed them.

Down in the farmyard Frog Eyes was still engrossed in his comic; he chewed nonchalantly on a carrot he had taken from a sack by the rainwater tank. Obviously Gilbert knew his way around Black Dog Farm quite well.

Wib scanned the nearby fields with Arthur's binoculars. He caught sight of another figure walking towards the farm, along the footpath from the main Devizes road. The focus wheel on the binoculars was a little stiff and Wib frantically fiddled with it in order to get a clear view of the new visitor.

The blurred image through the glasses gradually became sharp. Wib couldn't quite believe who he was looking at, so he fiddled with the focus wheel once more; but there was no mistaking who the visitor was. He hadn't seen him for over a year but it was him all right. It was Mr Harris, Wib's father.

Wib anxiously bit his nail as his father strolled confidently towards the farm and Old Stoopy. In his head all the things his mother had ever said about his father came back to him. ''Waster'' and a ''fly by night'' she always called him. On more than one occasion Wib could remember the police knocking on their door in Paxton Street. Mr Harris would quickly jump over the back wall that led to the house behind, and Joyce would be forced to go to the front door and lie about not having seen her father for ages. It wasn't a very nice thing to have to do, and it always upset Joyce.

There was also the time he frightened the life out of them by arriving home, out of breath, with his leg bleeding from a nasty dog bite. His case had burst open and spilled its contents of alarm clocks all over the kitchen. The others could never work out why they needed so many alarm clocks. But Wib knew they were stolen. Mr Harris stayed in the garden shed for a week, having his meals brought to him by the children—who were all scared of catching some unpleasant disease from the ugly bite on his leg.

When he'd walked out on them a year ago Mrs Harris had seemed strangely unmoved. "We're lucky to be rid of him," she had said, and the children had appeared to agree with her.

From his position high on the hill, Wib could see P.C. Keogh and four local shopkeepers striding in the opposite direction, up Toe Lane towards Black Dog Farm. Arthur and Freddy followed at a distance; far enough behind to be safe and close enough to be nosey.

Mr Harris was carrying a leather case that looked very heavy, judging by the way he changed it over from hand to hand as he went along. What if it was filled with stolen goods to barter with Old Stoopy? Wib was unsure what to do; even if Mr Harris was a thief, he was still his father.

He put the binoculars back into their pouch and ran down the side of the hill towards the footpath. Mr Harris had his eyes firmly fixed on Black Dog Farm so he didn't see his son coming up behind him. Wib was frightened to get too close, and a good ten yards from his father he stopped and shouted out.

"D . . . d . . . ad."

Mr Harris spun round at the unfamiliar sound. He screwed up his eyes and examined the tiny figure standing at the side of the path.

"It's me, Dad, Wibby."

"Wibby? No it can't be."

Mr Harris put down his heavy case and frowned, puzzled, as if he didn't really believe what he was looking at.

"Well, I'm blowed. I don't believe it. Of all the people . . . I heard you was evacuated . . . but had no idea it was here. Come closer, let's have a look at you. Fancy that! All this way and who do I bump into but my own nipper." He beckoned Wib, but Wib stayed where he was.

"Come here, lad, don't be scared. It's only me . . ."

"You're not going to Black Dog Farm, are you, Dad?"

"That's right, lad, a bit of business with an

old pal of mine.'' Mr Harris patted his case. ''Buckshee . . . off the back of a lorry, if you get my meaning.''

He winked at Wib who knew his meaning all right. He was right. The contents of the case would almost certainly be stolen and of more than a passing interest to P.C. Keogh, who would be returning with Freddy and Arthur at any minute. His father would be caught red-handed, just like Stoopy and the Bootwicks.

''This pal of yours—he hasn't got a stoop has he?''

''That's right. Harry Benson. Do you know him?''

''No . . . it's just . . . Look, I've got to go now, my dinner will be ready.''

Wib began to run up the steep bank at the side of the footpath. Mr Harris called after him.

''Here, where you off to? Is your mother with you?''

''No. Just me, Fred, Vee and Joycie.''

''Hang on a minute, son, you haven't told me where you're staying, or anything. I'd like to see Joycie and the others before I get back.''

''Butt's House, Urchley Lane. I've got to go . . . Bye.''

Wib ran further up the bank and his father, picking up his case, continued on his way. He shook his head and smiled at his son's behaviour.

Wib stopped to look back. Mr Harris was

whistling "Umbrella Man"—his own favourite tune. What was he doing? This man was his father, he reminded himself. His own father. And he was sending him to be caught by the police. What kind of son was he? He wished he hadn't whistled that song, of all songs.

"Dad . . . Dad . . . don't go up there!"

Mr Harris stopped whistling and spun round.

"What? Up where?"

"To Black Dog Farm. There's coppers up there . . ."

"Coppers?" said Mr Harris, his friendly paternal face suddenly changing into the selfish thief Wib was more used to. "You sure?"

"Course I'm sure . . . it was us who shopped them."

Wib wasn't hanging around for a reply; he knew his father's temper only too well. He ran as fast as he could over the brow of the hill at Dingle's Piece and made for the high street. With luck Cyril would be in and he could hide there. Mr Harris dropped his case and tore up the hill after his son.

Over at Black Dog Farm, P.C. Keogh was frantically blowing his police whistle. With the help of Mr Belcher and Mr Noblock, he had managed to apprehend the burly Mr Bootwick and apply his policeman's arm-lock. He had been dying to do that for twenty years.

Mr Jerem who ran the George & Dragon pub had no trouble in subduing the frail Stoopy. It was sixteen stones against ten, and Mr Jerem's great arms—used to lifting heavy ale casks—applied a half-nelson that nearly twisted Old Stoopy's head off.

Arthur and Freddy appointed themselves unofficial deputies and stopped young Frog Eyes from sneaking off behind the cow sheds.

At the other side of Dingle's Piece, Mr Harris had caught up with Wib and grabbed him roughly by his scarf.

"Now listen here, Wib." Mr Harris panted hard, trying to get his breath back. "You listen to me, and listen good. I'll see you tonight. And remember you're to button your lip . . . else you'll be for it. Understand?"

Wib nodded.

"Not a word, right."

Wib nodded once more and Mr Harris twisted the scarf around his neck a little tighter.

"God's honour?"

"God's honour," replied Wib—and he meant it. Mr Harris ran back to the footpath to pick up his case and get back to the main Devizes road.

Wib loosened his scarf and ran towards Black Dog Farm, anxious to tell Freddy all about his meeting. But he knew he couldn't. This was one secret he couldn't even share with his brother.

CHAPTER 20
POOL

Wib knew every little detail of the religious paintings on the bedroom wall at Butt's House. They were dimly illuminated by the small pool of light thrown out by the hissing gas mantle, but if Wib screwed his eyes up he could see them quite clearly. Freddy sighed as he settled his head into a dip in the soft feather pillow. He had been very pleased with his game of cops and robbers—it was just like Saturday morning pictures—and consequently he had gone to sleep with a very contented smile on his face.

The painting Wib was looking at featured a man in chains at the gates of what looked like an English prison, except there was sand and palm trees everywhere. Another man with a beard and long white robes was unlocking the man's manacles, helped by a gang of ragged children. Underneath in black copperplate letters it said, ''Call not a man wretched who, whatever ill he suffers, has a child to love.''

In the dim light the man in chains looked a lot like his father. Wib pulled off the eiderdown and climbed out of bed. On closer inspection, however, it looked nothing like Mr Harris. In fact it was the spitting image of Syd Walker, the Wandering Junk Man.

Wib's ears pricked up as he heard the back

gate open in the yard. Turning down the gas, he tip-toed to the window and gently pulled back the thick curtain. He wasn't surprised to see his father. Mr Harris spotted Wib almost at once and motioned to him to come down into the yard. Wib shook his head.

"I can't," he whispered through the glass. "I'm not allowed."

"Get down here right away." Mr Harris spat through the gaps in his brown teeth as he spoke.

Wib put on his coat and slipped down the secret staircase, and out into the side field.

"I'm here, Dad."

Mr Harris turned around, surprised at his son's arrival from the opposite direction.

"How d'you get here? You didn't come out the door."

"There's a side door."

"Right. Come over here." Mr Harris pointed at Mr Bixey's locked-up petrol shed. "I smell petrol. Am I right?"

Wib nodded.

"Yes. A lot of it. Miss Doughbridge, the lady in the house, she's got three farms and keeps all the petrol for the tractors in here."

Mr Harris rattled at the lock.

"Bugger. It's locked."

"There's a key."

"Where?"

"Mr Bixey keeps it."

"Get it!"

"I can't. He lives in the other house."

"Get it!"

"But he keeps it on his watch-chain."

Mr Harris wasn't going to take no for an answer. He raised his voice as loudly as he dare.

"Get it!"

The back door of Butt's Farm was never locked and Wib simply lifted the latch and walked straight in. Mr Bixey didn't hear Wib on the creaky staircase, but Jip did. From the darkness of the landing he growled menacingly at the intruder.

"It's all right, Jip boy," whispered Wib. "It's only me. It's Wibby—there's a good boy. Easy now. Easy boy."

Wib stroked the dog to calm him. Jip licked Wib's face and then gently padded back into his corner.

Mr Bixey's door catch was loose and it rattled as Wib opened it. Every tiny noise was exaggerated inside Wib's head, and each floorboard seemed to creak as he tip-toed across the bedroom. Mr Bixey had spent the evening at the George & Dragon and was snoring loudly in his bed. He was not the neatest of people and his clothes were strewn haphazardly across the floor. Wib found his waistcoat lying across a chair under the window, and very carefully he pulled the watch-chain out from the fob-pocket. Mr Bixey stirred in his sleep and shook his fat cheeks before turning his face to the wall. Wib unclipped the petrol shed key from the chain and tip-toed back to the stairs—patting Jip on the head as he went.

Downstairs in the yard, Mr Harris snatched the key from Wib and undid the lock hanging from the tie-bar. The fumes from the shed made Wib feel bilious and he stood by the open door to get some fesh air. Mr Harris handed him a torch.

"Hold this . . . and for goodness sake, close the door."

Wib pulled the door to and flicked the torch switch on.

From his case Mr Harris took a strange contraption that looked like a number of gas-masks hooked up together.

"What's that?" asked Wib.

"This stuff's not regular petrol, it's Pool. I've got to filter out the dye."

"Pool. What's Pool?"

"It's petrol—coloured pink. Special for farmers. If you get caught selling it in London it's the nick with no trouble. So I'm going to filter it through here, see, then the petrol's got no colour. I can flog it where I want then, and no one knows where I got it from. Hold the torch over here, so I can see."

Wib pointed the torch once more at the crude filtering apparatus as, one by one, Mr Harris emptied the jerry-cans into the funnel.

Wib was getting sleepy and yawned, causing the torch beam to drop.

"Wib! Watch what you're doing."

"Sorry . . . Dad."

It was funny calling him "Dad". He didn't really want to. He didn't really want to be there at all. Outside Wib heard another voice.

"Hello. Who's there? Wib, is it you?"

"It's Joycie!"

Mr Harris snatched the torch out of Wib's hands.

"Go out and talk to her. Don't let her see me."

"What shall I say?"

"Say anything. Keep her out."

Wib slipped out into the yard. Through the darkness he could see Vee and Joyce standing by the farm gate. They had their coats over their shoulders, but were shivering all the same.

"Wib, is that you? What are you doing?"

"Nothing, really. Nothing at all."

Wib walked towards his two sisters to discourage them from looking any closer.

"Nothing? You must be doing something?"

"I'm not. Go in please, Joycie. I'll tell you about it in the morning. Please don't come any closer. Go back to bed . . ."

Wib didn't say any more because he was

interrupted by a loud whooshing sound as a huge sheet of flame shot out from the petrol shed.

"It's Dad!" shouted Wib. "He's in there."

Mr Harris stumbled out, his jacket on fire. He threw himself on the ground and rolled over in the puddles to put it out, shouting at the three children.

"Get out of here before the whole lot goes up!"

Wib, Vee and Joyce ran back into the farmyard and ducked down behind the stone wall.

"What's he doing here?" said Joyce.

"He just turned up. He was after Doughbridge's petrol. He must have made a spark or something."

"Are you there, Dad? What's happening?"

Mr Harris coughed and spluttered, dragging himself out of the muddy puddle. He took one last look at the blazing shed and ran off into the night. It was just in time, because at that moment there was another explosion and the flames leapt in the air, throwing sparks and burning rafters everywhere. The flames lit up the sky and Mr Harris could clearly be seen scurrying across Butt's Field. He obviously had little concern for the safety of his children, and limped badly from his own burns.

"Dad! Where are you going?" shouted Joyce. "Where are you going?"

"Let him go. Don't say nothing. Don't say nothing at all," shouted Wib.

"Why?"

"'Cause I said God's honour not to tell."

"But why?"

"'Cause he's our dad, that's why. Now you say God's honour, as well."

"But what for, Wib?"

"Say it!"

"God's honour," repeated the two girls.

They weren't sure what Wib was on about but it seemed to put his mind at rest.

"Look!" Vee had turned towards Butt's Farm and noticed, to her horror, that the roof thatch had caught fire.

Mr Bixey ran across the yard in his pyjamas and Jip barked loudly at his heels. Freddy had also arrived at the door, closely followed by Miss Liggerty in her nightgown. Mr Bixey pumped at the old metal handle of the water pump to fill a bucket, but it was hopeless. The flames had already spread from barn to barn and were now creeping along the roofs to Butt's House itself.

"Mr Bixey, help me, please," shouted Miss Liggerty. "We've got to get Miss Doughbridge."

Bixey yelled at the children who stood transfixed, staring at the enormous blaze—it was just like the fire bombs in Paxton Street.

"Get out of here, you young 'uns. Get in the lane out of the way." The children obeyed immediately and ran out of the gate.

"What started it?" asked Freddy. "Is it a

bomb?''

''We'll tell you later. Belt up,'' Wib snapped back at his bewildered brother.

Bixey and Liggerty helped the limping Miss Doughbridge out into the yard. Joyce and Vee smiled to themselves at her comical nightgown and long night-time plaits. Cane and Abel scooted along the narrow wall away from the flames. Chickens ran around everywhere, already burned out of their coops.

Mr and Mrs Gubber arrived from Frogshitch Farm to help, but there was nothing anyone could do. By now the flames had taken a firm hold and were systematically gobbling up the rafters; they licked out of every window at both Butt's Farm and Butt's House. Miss Doughbridge was so overcome she had to be sat down. Mrs Gubber put her coat round her and persuaded her to go back to Frogshitch Farm.

The children watched helplessly as the home they'd got to know, but never love, went up in black smoke. Poor old Wilf Bixey watched with different feelings. He had lived with his wife Fay for twenty years at Butt's Farm and, in the space of a month, he had lost them both.

CHAPTER 21
SIX MONTHS

Joyce had a horrible feeling she'd been through it all before. Being burned out wasn't very different to being bombed out—it left you without a place to live and you always seemed to end up in a school hall. This time it was the Pottley school hall, much smaller than Larkwood Street, Hackney. It was no more than twenty feet square but on a Sunday morning, seated as they were on a low bench in the middle, the hall looked bigger than it ever had. The emptiness of the room made their voices echo and words seemed to drift upwards, so that conversations appeared to take place somewhere up in the rafters.

Everywhere was spotlessly clean and the air was thick with the smell of carbolic. Through the glass partition they could see Mrs Knapp-Jenkins, the billeting officer, deep in conversation with Miss Godball, their teacher, Mrs Noblock, P.C. Keogh, Mr Bixey and Mrs Spicer. The four children could see their mouths moving, but the glass was thick enough to hold back the sounds. It was funny, Joyce thought, like watching a silent film at the "Tuppenny rush" cinema in Hackney. Except these people were real and the words they spoke were about her.

After the fire, Miss Liggerty and Miss

Doughbridge had been treated for shock at Devizes Infirmary and stayed overnight at the Bear Hotel. The children had been put up briefly at Frogshitch Farm, and now sat quietly in the school hall awaiting their fate.

"There's a Waifs and Strays Home," said Vee, breaking the silence.

"A what?"

"A Waifs and Strays Home."

"Where?"

"Seagry Manor—other side of Devizes. Doreen told me all the orphans go there."

"We're not orphans!" countered Wib, rather annoyed.

"Well, we are, sort of . . ."

"We're evacuees, stupid, it's quite different. Orphans is when you've got no one."

"We're like orphans. We've got no mum. She's in London—and God knows where Dad is . . ."

"You're not to say anything about him! You said 'God's honour'." Wib was beginning to get angry. Being called an orphan upset him, and any mention of Mr Harris broke the pact the children had secretly made, not to tell a soul about the petrol and their father's intentions.

Mr Bixey had put the fire down to some chemical fertilizer he had kept in the shed. "Gone rotten and exploded," he had said, but they all knew differently.

"Joycie, tell her to shut her trap up, will you," said Wib.

"Belt up, Vee," Joyce said firmly, but quietly. "We're not orphans at all. They'll have to find us somewhere else to live. It's the law."

"As long as it's not with Drawbridge," said Wib.

"It won't be," answered Joyce abruptly, annoyed at losing her concentration.

She was still trying to work out the words Mrs Knapp-Jenkins was mouthing behind the partition.

"Doughbridge and Liggerty are going to a place called Weston-Super-Mare, to a hotel for conva . . . convalescence. Mr Bixey told me."

Joyce's tongue tripped over the difficult word.

"What's that? Will it kill 'em?" asked Wib hopefully.

"It's to make them better."

"Pity."

"What's happening to poor Mr Bixey?" Vee asked the question, but didn't get an answer because Mrs Knapp-Jenkins and the others came out into the hall.

"Well, children . . . I expect you're feeling a bit peckish, so Mrs Noblock has kindly invited you to lunch." This piece of news made them all smile; grocers' wives always had full larders.

"We've decided to write to your mother,"

Mrs Knapp-Jenkins continued, "to tell her the news. She's not on the telephone and a telegram will only worry her unnecessarily."

"What about a new house, miss?" asked Wib politely. "Where do you reckon we'll be living?"

"Well," answered Mrs Knapp-Jenkins, "it's not easy. As you know, the houses in Pottley are very cramped and not everyone is . . . well, keen to take evacuees . . ."

"We won't have to go to the Waifs and Strays Home, will we, miss?" Freddy got his question off his chest. The very sound of a 'Home' filled him with dread. In Hackney he'd heard too many horrible stories about the workhouse.

"Only we haven't got nits," Wib added, "and we're not orphans, so we don't really want to go to a home . . ."

"Or have our hair shaved off!" said Freddy. "We wouldn't like it at all."

"In fact we'd hate it."

Mrs Knapp-Jenkins smiled one of those sickly smiles that professional 'do-gooders' with double-barrelled names always seem to have permanently stuck to their faces.

"No, of course you won't be going to a home —in fact these kind people here have agreed to take you." She gestured to Mrs Noblock and Mrs Spicer.

"What all of us?" asked Vee quickly.

"Well, you'll have to split up, I'm afraid. Mrs Noblock has agreed to take you, Vee—you can squeeze in with young Doreen. Wib and Freddy, well Mrs Spicer's Eric is going into the army, so there's a spare room for the two of you . . ."

"Except when he's home on leave . . ." added Mrs Spicer, "then we'll make you up a bed in the front shop."

The very thought of spending the night in the middle of a barber's shop brought a faint smile to Wib's down-turned lips.

"But what about Joycie?"

Mrs Knapp-Jenkins put her papers away into a small attaché case before she continued in a friendly, but matter-of-fact way.

"Well, Joyce is a bit more difficult. She'll be in full-time employment, a job that is, come Easter and Mr Austin at the Palace has asked if she'd like to be an usherette. He's suggested that you lodge with his sister Rita, who has a small flat above the box-office—so it will be very handy for work. How does that sound, Joyce? Acceptable?"

"Oh, yes, miss . . ." It was more than acceptable. Actually having a flat *inside* a cinema was more than she could have dreamed of.

"I should say so. It'll be like living with Clark Gable!"

The next six months were the best the Harris children spent at Pottley. In fact, quite probably it was the best time they'd ever had anywhere.

Freddy and Wib were just four shops away from Vee at Noblocks the grocers, and they had settled in nicely with the Spicers. On a Friday when almost the whole village came in for a haircut, the three boys would make themselves busy in the shop, sweeping up the cut hair and putting the towels in the steam cabinet; and on one occasion Wib was allowed to hold the wax taper while Mr Spicer singed a customer's hair. There were all the usual games at Nubbley Edge, Dead End Gate and Cuffley Elbow.

They would take it in turns to be Squadron Leader Bigglesworth D.S.O., but more often than not it was Wib. Somehow he never got to be Algy or Ginger.

Even familiar places seemed more enjoyable without "Frog Eyes" Bootwick around. It made Wib roar with laughter when he heard Gilbert had been evacuated to his uncle, who ran a pub in Penzance. Now Frog Eyes would know what it was like to be in a strange place, far from home. When he thought about it some more, he felt rather sorry for him, and wished he hadn't laughed. It was no fun having a dad in prison.

Vee loved every second of living with the Noblocks. She'd even got to like Mrs Noblock's weak cocoa. But best of all she liked serving in the grocer's shop after school. Vee always dreamed of working in Woolworths when she was older and it was heaven to be given jobs like tying tuppenny bundles of wood, crossing off the coupons in the ration books, or piling up the packets of Soako and Glitto on to the shelves.

Joyce had a marvellous six months also, surrounded by Claudette Colbert and Rita Hayworth. It had been strange at first without the others but she got on well with Rita Austin, who she lodged with, and slowly she had begun to enjoy her independence. It was almost like being a grown-up. She'd even got quite adept at handling the cheeky remarks from the young soldiers of the Wiltshire Regiment, as she showed them to their seats at the Palace.

Twice a week she would visit Wib, Freddy and Vee at Pottley. Having a regular wage packet meant she could buy them all an occasional luxury like a bar of Rowntree's—when she could get hold of it. Wib never stopped being pleased at having a big sister who actually earned money. It made him feel very proud.

Joyce also visited Mr Bixey, who had managed to get a job at Mill Farm and a permanent room over at the George & Dragon. Mr Jerem had even allowed Jip to stay. Being over a pub made it very handy for him to indulge in his favourite, and now, only pastime, which was exercising the arm he raised his pint glass with. Every time Joyce visited him his stomach seemed to have got larger and his cheeks rosier. He always seemed jolly enough but Joyce knew that his loneliness was hidden deep inside him, and the ready smile was only there by courtesy of Wadsworth's Best Bitter.

Helping the farmers cutting the corn, threshing and bundling, was another new pleasure for Vee, Wib and Freddy. But Vee became very upset as the patch of uncut corn got smaller and smaller, and the rabbits began their desperate dash for freedom. The farmer's guns made easy work of popping them off, and very soon there were thirty or more dead rabbits hanging upside down from the fence. Both the Spicers and Noblocks had rabbit stew for weeks.

Fruit picking was another delight. Freddy and Wib would walk down the strawberry patch, bent over double, filling their faces with strawberries that were plump, fresh and, above all, free. As they walked they would sing "All good things around us are sent from heaven above." This would put them in good stead if the vicar spotted them, but wouldn't cut any ice at all if they were caught by the farmer.

CHAPTER 22
MR CHURCHILL SAYS . . .

Joyce was the first to get the letter. She was handed it one morning by Mr Austin who had come in early to do his books. Ronald Colman in *Under Two Flags* had been packing them in and he expected a profitable week.

The envelope was addressed to "Joyce Harris c/o The Palace Cinema, Market Place, Devices, Wilts."

She recognised the handwriting and, anyway, Devizes had been spelled wrongly, so it could only be from her mother. She ripped the envelope open with her thumb and sat on the arm of the settee to read it.

My Dear Joyce,

Marvellous news—we've managed to get a big flat—Peabody Buildings in Shoreditch—very good nick and Uncle Stanley has been doing it up something lovely and we've been saving up our coupons for some new bits and pieces—utility of course but nice—nothing too fancy. Also the bombing seems to be over, we haven't had a bad raid for weeks and Mr Churchill says—on the wireless—we've been through the worst of it—thanked us Londoners personal he did. And so with the flat and all, Uncle Stanley says he'd like you all to come home—and so would I of course. So I've written to Mrs Spicer and Mrs Noblock to tell them the good news. I'm so happy Joycie, it will be lovely to have us all together as a family again and Uncle Stanley is such a nice kind man I know you're going to like him. Oh well, will be in touch again soon, when I've sorted out all the odds and sods.

Lots and lots of love, T.T.F.N.

Mum

P.S. Siddy sends his love. He's done you all a drawing (enclosed). He's a big boy now and talks about you all the time—especially you Joycie. Must go now—trying to catch the last post.

Love again,

Mum

Joyce unfolded Siddy's drawing. There were lots of ack-ack guns, sandbags, explosions and a scribble with a swastika on its side to denote a German bomber exploding. It should have made Joyce feel homesick but it didn't. It conjured up a world that she'd forgotten existed and she wasn't at all sure if she wanted to go back to it.

Mrs Noblock called Vee and Doreen into the front room over the grocers shop and read the letter out loud.

"Does that mean I have to go home, Mrs N?"

"'Fraid so, lovey."

"But the war's not over yet!" Doreen protested. "And she likes it here."

"We'll miss you, lovey," said Mrs Noblock, sadly. Vee didn't answer. She opened her book of flower pressings and silently flicked through it. There was a memory of the countryside pressed between each page. She felt a lump creep up inside her throat and her eyes moistening. But she was determined not to cry. She couldn't. After all, going home ought to be a happy occasion.

Mrs Spicer couldn't bring herself to tell Wib and Freddy the contents of her letter, and handed the job over to her husband.

"I think Mr Spicer's got something to tell you boys if you'd like to pop down the shop," she said, as she cleared away their breakfast things.

Mr Spicer was giving one of his customers a "short back and sides". He had his back to the boys but saw them reflected in the mirror as they came down the stairs.

"Sharpen my razor, will you, boys. Mind how you go, though. Carefully does it."

The boys couldn't believe their ears. Sharpening Mr Spicer's cut-throat razor was the plum job in the shop and it usually went to young "Ciggywig" Cyril.

Freddy got there first and lifted up the leather strap that hung from the wall; he pulled it taut. Wib took the open razor and carefully stroked it up and down on the smooth surface.

Mr Spicer picked up a small hand-mirror and showed his customer the back of his hair.

''O.K. for you, sir?''

''Oh, ah. Very nice,'' replied the customer, in a gruff Wiltshire accent. Then Mr Spicer, almost as if he was continuing the conversation with the man, broke the news to the boys.

''Oh, by the way, boys, your mum's wrote us a letter. She's making arrangements for you to be going back to London.'' He then casually went back to talking about the weather with his customer.

Wib and Freddy stopped honing the steel razor. Freddy was so taken aback by the news that he looked up and almost cut himself with the sharp edge. Wib quietly walked to the door and out into the street. Freddy shouted at him through the painted window.

''Where you going?''

''Cuffley Elbow.''

''Now?''

''Now!''

''Why?''

'''Cause it might be our last chance, stupid!''

Freddy threw the razor into the basin and dashed after Wib across the high street. Mr Spicer watched them turn the corner at the post office, into Urchley Lane. He took his handkerchief out from his waistcoat pocket. It hadn't been very nice telling them the news and he wasn't nearly as casual about it as he had pretended. He sneezed loudly into the handkerchief. Hairs up the nose were one of the hazards of being the village barber.

The Great Western steam train was blackened by the dirt and smoke of a thousand journeys. The engine's giant wheels locked together as it strained to pull the six maroon coaches out of Devizes Station. Wib, Freddy, Vee and Joyce squeezed their heads out of the narrow corridor window to wave goodbye. They fiddled awkwardly with their gas-mask cases—it was so long since they'd carried them.

Cyril and Arthur ran along the platform, keeping level with their window, closely followed by Doreen who, in her own way, wobbled after them. They carried on until they reached the end of the platform and could run no further. Doreen waved so hard she thought her arm would drop off. From the train her dumpy body, Arthur's moley face, Cyril's pink cheeks, Mr Bixey, the Spicers and the Noblocks shrank in size, until the engine turned behind the hill and they all disappeared—forever.

It was nice to be upstairs in the front seat of a double-decker bus again, but it was a grey journey from Paddington to Peabody Buildings, Shoreditch. Out of the windows there were grey smoky ruins, everywhere queues of grey-clothed people with matching grey expressionless faces.

Wib noticed a familiar landmark in the Salvation Army Hostel, where for two pence you could go to "The Happy Hour" sing-songs and watch slides of missionaries. If you were really lucky you'd catch sight of some native ladies with their bras off. But it all seemed boarded up now.

The cream and green tiles that lined the staircase up to the new flat had been recently cleaned, and there was no doubt their new home was a big improvement on Paxton Street. Vee leaned over the balcony wall and noticed an enormous corkscrew hop-scotch drawn in the playground, crying out for her expert attention.

Uncle Stanley ushered them into the front room and flipped the china top off of a bottle of R. White's Cream Soda.

"Champagne O.K., everyone?" Mrs Harris laughed nervously at Uncle Stanley's joke. "Bet you must be parched—come on in—don't be shy—take your coat off—make yourself at home—it *is* your home."

Siddy smiled shyly at Joyce and then went back to his toy crane to hide his embarrassment.

Wib and Freddy quietly looked around the tiny crowded room, and out of the window. The hard, black tarmac below was criss-crossed by a hundred different washing lines. Somehow it just didn't compare with the soft green open spaces at Cuffley Elbow or the steep hill at Dingle's Piece. Wib could still taste Mrs Spicer's treacle toffee in his mouth and even a sip of R. White's Cream Soda, however delicious, did nothing to erase the memory.

Freddy's thoughts were slightly on the brighter side. London after the blitz would be a paradise amongst the bombed ruins for anyone with a sharp eye for mischief and a blind eye for the "Keep Out" signs. There were a million secret hide-aways; bombed-out, over-grown churches and fenced-off hidden playgrounds where you could play for days without any grown up sharing your private world.

But most of all, they were home. Joyce picked up Siddy and hugged him to her as hard as she could. Vee unhooked her gas-mask, pulled off her coat, and emptied a box of dominoes on to the table.

"Wib? Freddy? Who wants a game?"

"Me," answered Freddy, for once thinking quicker than his brother. Wib picked up Siddy's cardboard toy box and fished out a handful of old dog-eared picture cards. He sat down in the new armchair to scrutinize the information on the backs. Things weren't so bad. They had a smart redecorated flat, with shiny new furniture and bright, clean wallpaper. They even had the nice prospect of a brand new dad, who seemed to like their mum.

All in all, the last year had been a happy one for the Harris children. They had been safe from the destruction of the blitz, and forever would have memories, mostly fond, of the lush, green countryside—and the puddles in the lane.

Glossary

Ack-Ack Gun: *Anti-aircraft gun (Anti-aircraft Command).*

Anderson Shelter: *Simplest and most popular shelter against heavy bombing. Made of curved steel dug into ground, it could withstand anything but a direct hit. Designed by William Patterson and named after Home Secretary Sir John Anderson. 2½ million supplied.*

A.R.P.: *Air Raid Precaution.*

Balaclava Helmet: *Woollen head gear resembling a Norman knight's chain-mail helmet. Keeps ears warm. Originally knitted by housewives for soldiers in the Crimean War.*

Beano: *Beloved comic published since 1938. Featured Lord Snooty and his pals, Big Eggo, Rip Van Wink, and many more.*

Billeting Officer: *Person responsible for finding accommodation for evacuees. People would often pretend to be out when they called.*

Blackmarket: *As most foods and goods were rationed there was a thriving illicit "under the counter" market. More often than not it was a friendly bartering of goods.*

British Bulldog: *A traditional playground game. Two teams line up opposite one another in single file. Front members fold arms and hop towards one another attempting to knock opponent off balance. Side with most members left hopping, wins.*

Bunny: (*rabbit*) *Cockney slang for excessive chatter. As in "too much bunny and not enough donkey". (Too much talk, not enough work.)*

Cats Cradle: *Game played on hand with piece of string, knotted to form a circle. Various patterns are formed by partner taking string from hands without disturbing original 'cats cradle'.*

Dandy: *Sister (or brother) comic to* Beano, *started in 1937. Favourite characters: Korky the cat, Desperate Dan, Keyhole Kate.*

Five-Stones: (*Sometimes called Cobs, Gobs, Jacks, etc.*) *Traditional kerbside game played by throwing small stones up in the air and catching them on the back of the hand. Several variations of game including "Lobsters", "Crabsies", "House that Jack Built" etc.*

Gas-Mask: *A respirator for protection against expected poison gas attacks. Consisted of a rubber face mask with a transparent visor and a round can-shaped filter at front. Faithfully carried everywhere by everyone (generally in buff cardboard box), but thankfully never needed.*

Hokey-Cokey: *Traditional working class party dance. Performed by a group of people, in a circle, involving various hand and leg movements. A sort of cross between "Ten green bottles" and "Knees up Mother Brown".*

Hotspur: *Popular comic started September 1933. Intellectual reading compared with* Dandy *and* Beano. *Mixed comic strip with written stories. Featured Smuggy of Red Circle School, Pep Talk Polonius, Codger Coggins (the tramp with the old school tie), and many more.*

Jack Hulbert: *Popular music hall, radio and film leading man. Generally with wife, Cicely Courtneidge.*

Knock-Downs and Topsies: *Two games that could be played with picture cards (cigarette cards). In Knock-downs a number of cards are placed against a wall and other cards are individually flicked at them. Those knocked down are retrieved by flicker. With Topsies cards are flicked alternatively at wall by players until a flicked card manages to land on top of another.*

Penny Drinks: *Small sweetshops would have bottles of soft drinks lined up like a bar and for a penny a tiny thimble-full of delicious Tizer, Cream-soda, Vimto etc., could be purchased and downed in one, like a cowboy.*

Pig-Bin: *A metal refuse bin at the end of each street to encourage people to save food scraps, (potato peelings etc.), which could be used as animal fodder.*

Pool: *The name given for the solitary brand of petrol available at the outbreak of war. It sold for 1/6d. a gallon. Heavily rationed, and strictly controlled. Commercial petrol was dyed pink so as to ensure its proper use.*

Singeing: *The purpose of singeing the hair was to eliminate split ends. A wax taper was used to prevent intense heat and not burn the hair more than necessary.*

Spanish Wood: *Soft chewy piece of wood with liquorice flavour. Could be chewed for ages. (Consequently also called "Everlasting stick".)*

Sticky-Toffee: *Playground game similar to 'He' or 'Tag' where the person touched joins hands with the person who is 'It'. The more people touched the longer the chain becomes.*

T.T.F.N.: *Catch phrase of Tommy Handley's very popular radio show ITMA (It's That Man Again). Stands for Ta Ta For Now.*

Threepenny All-Off: *Rather severe haircut that was extremely practical but would win few awards at hairdressing competitions.*

Tuppenny Rush: *Cinema, presumably named after the entrance fee and the enthusiasm to gain the cheaper seats.*

Umbrella Man: *Song made famous by music hall artistes Flanagan and Allen.*

Warney Echo: (*Sometimes called "Donkey"*). *Playground game. A donkey's 'back' is made by the first team (approximately five members) linking together, head down, in file. The front member clings to the railings. The opposing team then endeavours to vault onto the donkey's back with the intention of collapsing the team underneath.*

Worms: (*i*) *Medical name: Tinea. A fungus which affects the scalp—hair becomes thin and scaly, skin breaks out in red circular patches. Often spread by pets.*

(*ii*) *Also Thread worm (Enterobius Vermicularis). Eggs of this parasite enter host in contaminated food or water.*

Acknowledgements

Thanks to Jack Rosenthal, my favourite writer, who – writes much better evacuee stories than I do. To Norman Longmate whose marvellously detailed references, ferreting into people's memories, make films and books like this so much easier to do.
To Miss Green in the Devizes Public Library.
To Alan Marshall and Val who never get any credit for sorting me out. To Hilary on Keyboards.
To Lucy, Alexander, Jake and Nathan who sat patiently through each chapter when they would have sooner been watching the Six Million Dollar Man.
To Graham Tarrant whose idea the book was and who performed miracles with his semi-colons. To Bill (Wib), Elsie, Jim and Fred who, over the years, told me all the things Norman Longmate left out.

GAMES & PASTIMES

0352 Star

300027	**BACKGAMMON** Prince Obolensky and Ted James	£1.25
398124	**BEGINNING BACKGAMMON** Tim Holland	95p*
300574	**HOW I PLAY SNOOKER** Joe Davis	80p

0426 Universal/Tandem

175077	**CROSS-FIGURE PUZZLES NO. 1** L. G. Horsefield	50p
172248	**CROSS-FIGURE PUZZLES NO. 4**	50p
169425	**CODEWORDS NO. 3** 'Crosswords Ltd.'	45p*
169778	**FILL-IN PUZZLES NO. 1** Jean Andrew (Editor)	45p*
172590	**FILL-IN PUZZLES NO. 2**	45p*
172833	**FILL-IN PUZZLES NO. 3**	45p*
169697	**HIDDEN NUMBERS NO. 1**	45p*
17240X	**HIDDEN NUMBERS NO. 2**	45p*
169506	**HIDDEN WORDS NO. 1**	45p*
172329	**HIDDEN WORDS NO. 2**	45p*
164083	Norman Sullivan **SULLIVAN'S I.Q. TESTS**	50p
032950	**SULLIVAN'S 1ST BOOK OF CROSSWORDS**	60p
028821	**SULLIVAN'S 2ND BOOK OF CROSSWORDS**	60p
174941	**SULLIVAN'S 6TH BOOK OF CROSSWORDS**	50p
176383	**SULLIVAN'S 8TH BOOK OF CROSSWORDS**	50p
158431	**TANDEM'S 1ST QUIZ BOOK** S. Mason	40p

0427 Trophy

002001	Jean Andrew (Editor) **HIDDEN WORDS NO. 3**	50p*
000130	**LEADERGRAMS** (In association with Ideal Home)	50p
000017	**SULLIVAN'S 9TH BOOK OF CROSSWORDS** Norman Sullivan	50p

† For sale in Britain and Ireland only.
* Not for sale in Canada.
◆ Film & T.V. tie-ins.

TARGET STORY BOOKS

Adventure

	Gordon Boshell			
113918	**THE BLACK MERCEDES**			60p
114043	**THE MILLION POUND RANSOM**			60p
117468	**THE MENDIP MONEY-MAKERS**			60p

Animal Stories

	Molly Burkett			
118502	**FOXES, OWLS AND ALL**	(NF)	(illus)	70p
111567	**THAT MAD, BAD BADGER . . .**	(NF)	(illus)	35p
	Constance Taber Colby			
109899	**A SKUNK IN THE FAMILY**	(NF)	(illus)	45p
	I. J. Edmonds			
20011X	**LASSIE: THE WILD MOUNTAIN TRAIL**			60p
	G. D. Griffiths			
113675	**ABANDONED!**		(illus)	50p
	David Gross			
117549	**THE BADGERS OF BADGER HILL**		(illus)	50p
	Michael Maguire			
118774	**MYLOR, THE MOST POWERFUL HORSE IN THE WORLD**		(illus)	60p
	Joyce Stranger			
11017X	**THE SECRET HERDS**		(illus)	45p
110099	**THE HARE AT DARK HOLLOW**		(illus)	40p

Mystery And Suspense

	Ruth M. Arthur			
111648	**THE AUTUMN GHOSTS**		(illus)	50p
111729	**THE CANDLEMAS MYSTERY**		(illus)	45p*
	Tim Dinsdale			
105915	**THE STORY OF THE LOCH NESS MONSTER**		(illus)	50p
	Leonard Gribble			
104285	**FAMOUS HISTORICAL MYSTERIES**	(NF)	(illus)	50p
	Alfred Hitchcock (Editor)			
117387	**ALFRED HITCHCOCK'S TALES OF TERROR AND SUSPENSE**			60p
	Mollie Hunter			
113756	**THE WALKING STONES**		(illus)	45p*
	Freya Littledale			
107357	**GHOSTS AND SPIRITS OF MANY LANDS**		(illus)	50p

† For sale in Britain and Ireland only.
*** Not for sale in Canada.**
♦ Film & T.V. tie-ins.

Wyndham Books are obtainable from many booksellers and newsagents. If you have any difficulty please send purchase price plus postage on the scale below to:

Wyndham Cash Sales,
P.O. Box 11,
Falmouth,
Cornwall

OR

Star Book Service,
G.P.O. Box 29,
Douglas,
Isle of Man,
British Isles

While every effort is made to keep prices low, it is sometimes necessary to increase prices at short notice. Wyndham Books reserve the right to show new retail prices on covers which may differ from those advertised in the text or elsewhere.

Postage and Packing Rate
U.K.
One book 22p plus 10p per copy for each additional book ordered to a maximum charge of 82p.

B.F.P.O. and Eire
One book 22p plus 10p per copy for the next 6 books and thereafter 4p per book. Overseas 30p for the first book and 10p per copy for each additional book.